PLAYING ROUGH

Amanda Love

Playing Rough
Copyright ©
2017 by Author Amanda Love. All rights
reserved.

amandalovewrites@gmail.com

amandaloveblog.com

www.facebook.com/a.love124/

Cover Art: Addendum Designs

Publisher's Note: This is a work of fiction.
Names, characters, places and incidents are a
product of the author's imagination. Locales and
public names are sometimes used for
atmospheric purposes. Any resemblance to
actual people, living or dead, or to businesses,
companies, events, institutions, or locales is
completely coincidental.

☐

For my bud, Claire. Love ya, chick.

Dawson

The last thing I expect to find when I'm called to a late-night disturbance is a drop-dead gorgeous blonde trying to break *into* the local prison, when most sane people would be trying to break *out*. But the biggest surprise of all is that I know her. In the last five years, Kaylee has blossomed from pretty high school junior to the most beautiful woman I've ever seen – a woman who not only steals my breath, but my self-control too. I should be focusing on the job, on finding out what's brought her to the gates of the prison and back into my life, but all I can think about is having her under me on soft sheets, while I brand her mine from the inside out.

Kaylee

Demanding entry into a maximum detention facility to see the father I never knew existed probably wasn't my smartest idea ever, especially when the cops show up in the tantalising shape of Detective Dawson Ford, who's more than capable of throwing *my* ass in jail. Dawson is no longer the skinny senior I remember from high school, but six-feet-five of mouth-watering hotness, and I want nothing more than to feel his lips on mine, his hands on my body, helping me forget the nightmare that is my life.
As the undeniable attraction between us catches fire, what should have been a simple quest for information quickly escalates into a deadly battle of wills, leaving my fate, and my life, in the hands of a ruthless monster. My father.

DAWSON

It's late when despatch puts out the call about a disturbance. Another half hour and I would've been heading home but as much as I want to, I can't ignore it. Apparently, a young woman is outside the gates of Stanislaus Correctional Facility causing a scene and demanding entry. Strictly speaking, the prison guards can't touch her while she's still outside the perimeter, so it's down to me, as the nearest available unit, to go check it out.

I call it in, turning the cruiser in the direction of the detention facility on the outskirts of town which is only about fifteen minutes from my current location. I don't turn on the blues, knowing I won't have to fight traffic at this time of night. I wonder why the fuck someone is trying to get *in* the place when most sane people want to break *out*. Probably some whack job protesting her man's wrongful imprisonment. Just what I fucking need! My plan of a beer or two while I wind down and watch the boxing on cable is evaporating.

Before long, I'm pulling up behind a black VW Golf which looks less like it's been parked and more like it's been abandoned at a random angle. The detention facility is in the middle of nowhere, for good reason, and it's just my cruiser and the other car on the long stretch of road. I climb out, my hand automatically going to the glock in my holster as I cautiously approach the other vehicle.

As I draw level I see that it's empty, so I walk on past and head toward the prison gates. As I get nearer I can see a woman sitting on the sidewalk that runs up to the prison security checkpoint, her head and shoulders slumped forward so that her blond hair obscures her face.

I raise my hand to the shadowy figures of the guards in the security box, a silent signal that I'll take care of the situation, before turning my attention back to the woman sitting on the ground.

For some reason, her down-beaten posture tugs at my heart, an unusual reaction as I'm not usually a soft-touch in situations like this. I've developed a healthy caution during the last five years on the force but there's something about the abject way the woman sits there that stirs something within me.

7

"Ma'am? You shouldn't be here," I say firmly, keeping my voice neutral and coming to a halt several feet in front of her.

She doesn't look dangerous, but emotional women can be unpredictable, as I have good reason to know, and I make sure to keep a little distance between us until I've got the measure of the situation.

Her head lifts and I literally feel the impact of her face all the way from my eyes down to my suddenly aching balls. She's the most beautiful woman I've ever seen with her pink bow of a mouth and high cheekbones. Even her bright blue eyes are captivating, despite being swollen from crying. But the biggest surprise of all is that I know her.

"Kaylee?"

She frowns at me, her empty gaze replaced with confusion as she looks at me, trying to figure out how I know her name.

I forget how much I've changed since high school so it's understandable that she wouldn't remember the awkward, skinny senior that she tutored in Math for a year. The beard is probably throwing her off as well, along with the fact that I've now filled out to fit my six-five height. My passion for boxing in my spare time has not only given me a fitness level I could only have dreamed of at high school, it's also given me a body that's honed and hard with muscle.

Kaylee was sure-bet straight A student back then, despite only being a sophomore to my senior. She was the perfect example of why stereotypes are dangerous, as her blond hair and blue eyes belied a sharp intelligence. I'm pretty sure I wouldn't have scraped through graduation without her help as Math was my weakest subject. She was a beauty back then but there was no ego about her and I liked the way she treated everyone the same, regardless of how they looked or where they came from.

She's matured from pretty to jaw-dropping, although she has a fragile edge to her now and I'm curious about what's put it there. She's lost the soft, tempting curves I tried not to notice five years ago, and I'm suddenly hit by an overwhelming urge to take her home and fill her up not only with a good meal but with my suddenly needy cock, branding her mine from the inside out.

My eyes drop to her lips and I wonder what they'd feel like, whether she would open up and let me taste her with my tongue. I give myself a mental shake, wondering what the fuck is wrong with me and trying to get my wayward thoughts under control along with my horny dick. I can't believe I'm having such an immediate and urgent reaction to Kaylee Kemp, the girl who used to sit at the kitchen table with me while she taught me the finer points of trigonometry.

"Dawson? Dawson Ford?"

My attention is brought back to the present as Kaylee's expression clears, recognition dawning on her face. She pushes herself to a standing position and I'm reminded how tall she is as I get a tempting eyeful of her long, tanned legs in what appears to be a cheerleading skirt. My cock swells at the thought of having those legs wrapped around me and I discreetly adjust myself.

"What are you doing here, Kaylee?" I ask, ignoring her question and trying to get my mind off the unsettling demands of my body and back to the situation at hand.

She looks at me and her face crumples as a fat tear rolls down her cheek. "I wanted to see him," she says, wiping away the tear and looking at me. "I don't know what else to do, where else to go. Everything is such a mess!"

Her words make no sense to me. "See who?"

"My father. He's in there." She points in the direction of the prison.

"Your father's in there?" I ask, unable to believe that the mild-mannered, church-going Mr. Kemp I remember could have possibly done anything to get himself locked up in Stanislaus. "We *are* talking about the same man, right? James Kemp? Accountant in Bakersfield?"

Another tear escapes down Kaylee's cheek and she shakes her head, pressing her lips together as if she really doesn't want to say the next words out loud. "No. My real father is Levin Sarado Ivanovich, and he's in there awaiting trial for...a lot of bad shit."

I look at Kaylee in disbelief and can't decide if she's mad or drunk. "Wait. You're telling me that Lev Sarado, ex-cop-turned-mob-boss, is your father? Why the hell would you think that?"

"Because it's written on my birth certificate. Jennifer and James Kemp weren't my real parents. They adopted me," she says flatly, as if she's still coming to terms with the truth herself.

"Wait, you said they *weren't* your parents?"

Kaylee swipes at the tears on her cheeks. "They were killed in a car wreck a little less than a month ago."

"Shit, Kaylee, I'm so sorry! What happened?" I ask, shocked.

Kaylee shrugs. "The coroner said that Dad had a heart attack at the wheel, ploughed straight into an oncoming truck. The truck driver was treated for broken bones and a concussion, but Mom and Dad were killed instantly."

I close my eyes, feeling her pain, having lost a parent myself not so long ago. "So, how did you end up here?"

"I found my birth certificate and adoption papers when I was sorting out Mom and Dad's legal affairs. Maria Campbell and Lev Sarado are my biological parents. Guess I was never supposed to know," she says, a bitter edge to her voice. "Now Mom and Dad are gone, I thought maybe it was time I met my real father."

"You've driven here from Bakersfield? Alone?" I ask, feeling weirdly protective. Anything could have happened to a beautiful woman like her, on the road on her own at night. "Are you mad? What if you'd broken down or gotten a flat or…"

"Yeah, well, excuse me if I'm not particularly rational, right now!" she snaps, her eyes holding a world of hurt.

It's hard for me to swallow the fact that the couple I knew back in high school weren't Kaylee's biological parents, so God knows how difficult it must be for her. "Listen, you can't stay here. You're lucky it was me that got the call, or you could've landed your own ass in jail."

"Like father, like daughter, huh?" Kaylee says, with the first glimmer of a real smile.

It does amazing things to her already beautiful face and I find myself smiling back. "Come on, let's get you out of here. You must be frozen." I say, indicating her short skirt and the top that, while not skimpy, molds far too closely to her breasts, which are still a delicious handful despite her slender frame.

"Are you arresting me?" Kaylee asks.

An image of her naked and handcuffed to my bed, springs to mind and I clear my throat before I speak. "Not tonight, sweetheart," I say, the endearment rolling off my tongue surprisingly easily. "Do you have anywhere to stay?"

She looks uncertain, biting at her lip as if she suddenly realises how far from home she is. Seeing her chew on her lip like that makes me want to run my tongue over it, soothing the area she's worrying with her teeth.

"I came here on a bit of an impulse," she admits, giving me a sheepish look. "I didn't really think about what I was going to do beyond trying to see my … Lev," she catches herself.

"Well, you're not driving home now." My protective instincts bristle at the thought of her driving anywhere on her own at this time of night. "You can stay with me tonight. Drive back in the morning after a good night's sleep." The words are out of my mouth before I fully consider the temptation of having her under my roof for the night.

"Oh, no. I couldn't …"

"You can, and you will," I override her arguments before she can articulate them, surprising myself with my insistence. "My shift is finished now so I was heading home anyway. Your car will be safe here. I'll have someone collect it and drop it to my place tomorrow morning." My tone leaves no room for argument.

"Okay. Thank you," she says, looking lost and vulnerable and my heart aches a little at her defeated tone.

The woman before me is a shadow of the Kaylee I remember, who was full of enthusiasm for life. The joy has been syphoned from her and I'm suddenly overwhelmed with a need to help her find the spark she seems to have lost.

Kaylee

It feels surreal being here now and I'm beginning to regret my impulsive decision to make the journey. I threw some clothes and toiletries into a rucksack and before I could talk myself out of it, I was on the way to Modesto.

I've spent the last month dealing with the fallout of my parents' deaths, making funeral arrangements and trying to get on top of the mountain of paperwork required to close the accountancy business Dad owned, not to mention the insurance policies and legal documents related to the house.

During this process, I learned that Jennifer and James Kemp adopted me when they were both in their forties, after trying unsuccessfully for years for a child of their own. They were almost a generation older than the parents of my best friend, Meri, and old-fashioned in their outlook and beliefs. I had a strict upbringing and although they were very protective, they weren't overly demonstrative and never hugged or kissed me in the way that Meri's parents do with her and her brother.

I envy Meri's relationship with her parents, how open and loving they are with each other. It's been one of the things I've wondered about since finding out I was adopted - why a couple would bring a child into their home if they weren't going to love me unconditionally.

There were so many signs that I missed, or maybe I just didn't want to see the differences between me and my parents. They were both dark haired with brown eyes and average height, whereas I'm five-ten with blonde hair and blue eyes. Seems so ridiculously obvious now that I wasn't their biological child but, prior to their deaths, I've never had a reason to question my parentage.

I've been rebelling with a vengeance since they died. I know Meri's been worried about my drinking and partying in the last month, just as I know I'm in denial about the whole tragic mess that is my life, trying to drown the pain at the bottom of a bottle.

A simple internet search, the day I discovered my birth documents, revealed my biological father's full name, along with the sordid details of his criminal activities and subsequent arrest by Modesto P.D. in an investigation headed up by

Detective Daryl Jacobs. He's awaiting trial, but it seems a guilty verdict is a mere formality.

I didn't really have a plan when I drove up here beyond finding the prison and demanding they let me in to see my real father. Pretty shitty plan and I knew I probably had more chance of growing a four-foot penis than being allowed in to see him, but my irrational mind was hell-bent on at least trying. I want to look my birth father in the eye to see if he really is the monster that everything I've read indicates.

At first, the two guards hadn't so much as batted an eyelid at my attempts to persuade them to let me in, but it wasn't long before it got ugly and the tears and shouting started. One of the guards had looked at me strangely, like I'd sprouted another head, while the other had called the cops.

Then just to put the cherry on top of the fantastic day I'm having, the cop that turns up is none other than Dawson Ford, the senior I tutored at high school. And, as Meri would say, 'holy-shit on-a-shingle he's hot!'

He was a looker even back then, but the gangly awkwardness of the senior I remember has been replaced with the quiet confidence of a man who's obviously risen quickly to the rank of detective. There wasn't an ounce of fat on him five years ago, but now he's buff, his arms and chest straining against the confines of his shirt. The beard is new, but it suits him, giving him a slightly edgy look and making me wonder how it would feel to have that beard softly scratching my skin as he kisses me.

I catch myself with a start, wondering at my wayward thoughts and realize I'm staring at him, a throb blooming to life between my legs as I lose myself in his deep brown eyes. A shiver which has nothing to do with being cold runs up my spine and I wrap my arms around my body, trying to conceal my suddenly-hard nipples.

Dawson lifts a hand in the security guards' direction as we turn and walk back toward the cars. I reach into the pocket of my skirt for my keys as we approach my VW, unlocking the trunk and pulling out the rucksack, throwing it over my shoulder.

"I need to drop the patrol car back to the station and pick up my car. My place is only a few minutes from there," Dawson says, as we climb into the cruiser and he cranks the engine. "So, what on earth made you think it was a good idea to just walk up to the prison gates and demand to be let in?" he asks, as we leave the prison behind.

"I don't know," I sigh, knowing it's a perfectly reasonable question. "I've been making a lot of crappy decisions lately. It's been a shit day and coming here was spur of the moment. I didn't think it through properly."

"What's with the outfit?" Dawson asks, indicating my clothing.

"California Cubs. NFL cheerleading squad."

"Ah, that's right. You used to cheer at high school. Sorry, football's not my thing," he says, shooting me an apologetic look. "I'm more of a boxing kinda guy."

"As in watching or doing?"

"Both. My friend, Tony, and I spar together, and he often comes to my place to watch the big pay-per-view matches."

"I don't know the first thing about boxing," I admit. "Cheerleading and football have been my life for the last two years. Not anymore, though. I was fired today."

"Why?" Dawson's eyes are full of genuine curiosity as he glances across at me.

I pause before answering, watching the car eat up the road in front of us, the countryside giving way to the more built-up areas of town. "Drinking, partying. Both of which I've been doing a little too hard of late, trying to forget…" my voice breaks, and I take a deep breath.

Dawson reaches across and places his warm hand over mine and I inhale sharply at the contact, feeling it all the way down to my toes and various other places in-between.

"Apparently my behavior was reflecting badly on the rest of the squad. Double standards because all the other girls do it, including the choreographer who fired me, and I know for a fact she's bumping uglies with two of the players. Veronica's always had a lot of influence over who stays and who goes on the squad and she's never liked me, so I guess I finally gave her the opportunity she was looking for."

Dawson glances across at curiously. "I never pictured you making a career out of cheerleading," he says, echoing my many conversations with Meri.

"The weird thing is, I'm not as upset about it as I should be. I mean, sure, I hate the double standards, but it was never my first choice of career."

"It doesn't hurt because it never really mattered," Dawson says, and I'm shocked at his perception. "What was your first choice?"

I hesitate, having only expressed my real ambition to Meri, and Mom and Dad. "Vet school."

Dawson nods, as if that's more in line with what he saw me doing. "So, why didn't you? There's a great vet school not far from here." He makes it sound so simple.

"I know. I made an application, thought I could maybe get a scholarship, but Mom and Dad were dead set against me coming here. I mean, they were always super protective, but I've never seen them so upset when I told them what I wanted to do, where I wanted to go. We had a huge argument and I told them I was going whether they liked it or not. We didn't speak for days. It all seems so...trivial now they're gone," I murmur.

"I'm so sorry about your parents, Kaylee. I remember how protective they were of you, but I'm surprised they encouraged you to settle for second-best. They didn't seem like the kind of parents that would hold you back."

Dawson's insight surprises me again. "You're right. So, why did they?" I frown as something occurs to me. "Maybe the real reason they didn't want me to come here was because they knew there was a chance I'd find out the truth."

"I guess only they could've answered that." Dawson says, casting me a sympathetic look as he turns the patrol car into the police station parking lot.

We climb out of the car and I follow Dawson to a black Corvette Stingray. "Nice wheels."

"Give me classic over modern any day. Restored her myself," he says, giving the hood a loving pat and I roll my eyes at the gesture. What is it with men and their weird obsession with cars?

He opens the door for me and I slide into the passenger seat. The smell of leather, and a purely masculine smell that's all Dawson, surrounds me. I bend forward to place my rucksack in the footwell, smiling to myself as I admit that this car is already growing on me too.

"I just need to go make a quick phone call." Dawson says.

I straighten up, not realizing that he's propped a muscular arm along the door frame as he leans down to talk to me and my movement brings my face to within a few inches of his. My breath hitches in my throat and my eyes drop instinctively to his mouth. I run my tongue over my suddenly dry lips, feeling as if an invisible thread is pulling my mouth closer to his, so close I can almost taste him…

"I…uh…I'll be right back." Dawson clears his throat, spinning on his heel and heading off across the parking lot toward the station.

I close my eyes, groaning as I drop my head back on the headrest behind me. I swear by all that's unholy that no man has ever got my panties in a twist like Dawson has in the last hour. What the hell is wrong with me? My experience with men may be limited but I'm not so green that I don't recognise full-blown lust when it hits me in the nether regions.

Is Dawson feeling it too? Or am I just imagining the heat in his eyes when he looks at me? Maybe I need to look a little lower to know for sure? Despite the attraction I feel for him, he's still incredibly easy to talk to. Who would've guessed that the guy I tutored five years ago would end up bailing me out in my time of need? I'm not surprised that he ended up becoming a cop as there was always a core of decency in Dawson that I recognised even back then, but he has a rougher edge to him now, like he's seen and done things that have honed the softer edges from him.

"All set." Dawson startles me from my thoughts as he slides behind the wheel. "As the shepherd said to his sheep, let's get the flock outta here," he grins.

"That's terrible!" I laugh, enjoying the feeling of lightness it brings. It seems like a long time since I've had anything to laugh about.

Dawson cranks the engine and a rich, throaty purr fills the air as we pull out of the parking lot. Within minutes Dawson takes a left at a gated community, pulling up in front of a two-storey house with a neat front yard and a wrap-around porch.

"This is your place?" I ask, impressed.

"All mine," Dawson replies. "I had some money left to me by my dad - I sure as shit couldn't have afforded it otherwise. Buying a house seemed like as good an investment as any."

"Dad always said that bricks and mortar is a better investment than any bank," I murmur, realizing that I haven't spoken about my Dad in that easy manner for weeks. "I guess that's why he and Mom made sure the house was in my name."

Dawson smiles. "Accountant through and through."

I grab my rucksack as we climb out of the Corvette and follow Dawson up the path to the front door. He pushes the door open, sweeping a hand in front of him to indicate I should go in first. A lamp on a table in the entranceway emits a welcoming glow and illuminates the space just enough that I can see the open plan living and dining area to my right, with what looks to be a modern kitchen beyond.

"Here, let me," Dawson says, closing the door and plucking the rucksack from my shoulder, "I'll show you to your room. I always keep the spare made up in case Mom comes for a visit. I'm sure you could use a shower and a change of clothes."

I follow him up the stairs, grateful for his thoughtfulness. The idea of a hot shower to wash away the day sounds like bliss.

He opens a door, flicking on the light switch to reveal a room tastefully decorated with cream and gold tones and a double bed. This room has benefited from a woman's touch and a pang of jealousy spears through me until I remember what Dawson said about it being his mom's room when she visits.

Dawson strides into the room and opens another door which leads into a small but impeccably clean bathroom. "This is your bathroom and there are clean towels in the cupboard there. Take your time. You wanna join me for a beer after or...?"

"A beer sounds great," I say quickly, still feeling jacked up from the day and knowing it will help me relax.

"Good." He hesitates, as if he wants to say more, but then seems to change his mind. "I'll leave you to it."

DAWSON

It takes every ounce of willpower I have to walk away from Kaylee, knowing there's a perfectly comfortable double bed right behind her. I must be a sick fuck, because not even the thought that it's where my Mom usually sleeps can calm the gnawing hunger that's escalating out of control where Kaylee is concerned.

The strength of the sexual attraction I feel for her is new to me. Sure, I've wanted women before, but never anything close to what I feel with her. I already feel possessive about her and I'm pretty fucking sure that doesn't bode well for me.

I head to my own room, needing a shower myself. My cock is hard as a rock despite turning the temperature to cold in an attempt to deflate the beast. But there's no taming it since I clapped eyes on Kaylee a few hours ago and with a sigh, I succumb to the need for release, taking my swollen shaft in hand as I imagine Kaylee's sweet lips wrapped around my throbbing length. I palm myself, dragging my hand up and down my shaft from root to tip and it seems like only a matter of seconds before I'm coming hard and fast, my release heightened by the images of the leggy blonde with blue eyes behind my eyes.

After drying off, I dress in jeans and a white t-shirt and head downstairs to grab two bottles of beer from the fridge.

Kaylee comes into the kitchen looking like a vision, despite being dressed casually in sweatpants and a tank top which molds to her amazing tits. Her face clean of makeup, her hair hanging down her back in wet tendrils and she looks beautiful. A flush creeps into her cheeks and I realize I'm staring at her like a gormless nerd with two bottles of beer dangling from my hands.

Recovering quickly, I hand one of the bottles to her, which she takes with a murmured thanks, before taking an impressive slug.

"Guessing you don't want a glass, then," I chuckle.

"Sorry. Not very ladylike I know, but there's something about drinking it straight from the bottle," she laughs. "Somehow, it doesn't taste the same when it's in a glass."

"You won't get any arguments from me," I agree, saluting her with my own bottle before lifting it to my mouth. "Come. Sit," I say, walking into the living area. "Make yourself at home." I indicate the sofa, watching her sink down and tuck her long legs underneath her before taking a seat at the other end.

I lean back, crossing my foot over my knee and resting an arm along the back of the sofa. "I guess it's been a rough time for you, not only losing your parents, but finding out you were adopted."

Kaylee takes another swig of her beer and leans against the cushion behind her with a sigh. "It's been a shock, to say the least. I know they loved me, but they were never very good at saying it or showing it. I was always trying to please them, win their affection by getting the best grades, the highest results, doing what they wanted rather than what was best for me."

"I'm sorry. I didn't know it was like that for you. I knew they were oddly protective of you by the way one or the other of them kept sticking their head round the door when we were studying. God knows what they thought we were up to!" Suddenly my mind is full of all the things we could've been up to back then. Kaylee flushes slightly and I wonder if she's thinking the same thing.

"You mentioned before that you were left some money by your father. Does that mean…?" She sees my frown and pauses. "I'm sorry, I didn't mean to pry."

The bite of grief is still fresh even after almost two years. "The cancer hollowed him out. I never thought I'd actually wish for him to die, for him to be out of pain and at peace."

Kaylee's eyes are full of sympathy as she places her hand over mine on the back of the sofa. "I'm so sorry, Dawson. I didn't know him well, but he seemed like a good man."

I thread my fingers through hers as if it's the most natural thing in the world. "He was the best father and friend a son could ask for," I say, my voice thick with emotion. "It's still hard to believe he's gone, that there's nothing left of him here."

"But there is," Kaylee says softly, her blue eyes holding mine. "You."

That one word hits me straight in the gut as my eyes roam over Kaylee's lovely face, drinking her in. I don't think I've ever seen anything as beautiful, her skin fresh and clean, her hair curling damply around her face.

Without breaking eye contact, I bring her hand to my mouth, placing a kiss against her palm. Not content with that brief, unsatisfying caress, I flick my tongue over the inside of her wrist, and the sound of her gasp at the simple caress has my cock fighting to get free. My eyes drop to the increased rise and fall of her breasts and the sight of her nipples hardening under my gaze unleashes something primitive within me.

I'm not sure who moves first, but our bodies and mouths come together in a heated rush. I've been dying for a taste of her since I laid eyes on her a few hours ago and her soft mouth is everything I imagined and more. I sweep my tongue inside, wanting more of the sweetness within and Kaylee moans, meeting the thrust of my tongue with her own and tasting me in return.

Fuck! I'm only kissing her and I'm about ready to shoot my load again. God alone only knows how amazing it would feel to submerge my throbbing shaft into her welcoming heat.

I tug her toward me, grasping her thighs so that she's straddling my hips. I move my hands to the hem of her top and she lifts her arms as I slowly peel it up and over her head and my eyes drop to the silky flesh I've revealed. Her glorious tits are just waiting for my mouth, her nipples rosy peaks begging for my tongue. I bring my mouth to within an inch of one of those hard, little nubs and pause, denying us both for just a few more seconds, drawing out the torture.

"Dawson!" Kaylee moans and shivers, arching her back in mute invitation, and the husky sound of my name on her lips is all I need.

Spreading one hand across her back, I pull her to me, my mouth enveloping her as I flick my tongue over one hard nipple, while my hand swallows her other breast, pinching lightly at the hard nub.

"Oh, God!" Kaylee chokes, tightening her thighs around me and pressing herself against the steely hardness barely contained by my jeans.

"You are so beautiful," I murmur, releasing her breast, biting and nibbling my way down her rib cage. "I've been wanting to do this from the minute I laid eyes on you at the prison."

"You have?" Kaylee's voice is breathless.

I look up, capturing her gaze with mine. "This...and much, much more."

Kaylee pushes her hands through my hair, sweeping her fingers around and along my jaw as she tests the softness of my beard. She leans forward, her mouth hovering above mine. "Me too," she says, her voice a whisper as she places her lips against mine, first softly, and then harder, groaning as her nipples brush against the material of my t-shirt.

All at once, there's far too much clothing between us and I break the kiss, ripping off my shirt and pressing Kaylee back into the sofa underneath me. Her legs wrap around my hips as I settle my weight between her thighs and she reaches up, pulling my head down to hers, reclaiming my mouth in a searing kiss. Her luscious breasts flatten against my chest and she moans as our bodies strain feverishly against one another, seeking an even deeper contact.

A sudden knock at the door causes us both to jump, the sound of our breathing harsh in the silence of the room.

"What the…?" I'm pissed, not only that someone is banging on my door past midnight, but also at what they've just interrupted. The knock comes again, louder this time, followed by a familiar voice.

"Dawson? It's Tony! I know you're up! I can see the light on!"

Oh, I'm up alright, but not in the way Tony means!

I drop my forehead to Kaylee's, trying to calm my body. "We're not finished here...not by a long shot," I promise, dropping a quick kiss on her mouth before standing and retrieving both of our shirts. I quickly pull mine over my head, watching as Kaylee does the same and almost groaning aloud with disappointment as she covers up those magnificent tits.

"I'll just be…" Cheeks burning, she bolts for the stairs, almost tripping over her own feet in her haste to escape. Another insistent knock prevents me from following her and with a frustrated sigh, I stride to the door, throwing it open with a scowl.

"About time!" Tony grumbles, the older man not waiting for an invitation as he strolls past me. "I just picked up your message and came straight over," he says, collapsing onto the sofa with a sigh and giving me an expectant look.

"Prick," I mumble under my breath, and head to the kitchen to grab him a beer, along with another for myself.

Tony's been my mentor since I joined the force and I wouldn't have made detective so quickly without his support. He and I have become good friends over the last five years, sharing a passion for all things boxing, and despite my bad temper at his interruption, I have a lot of respect for the other man.

I hand Tony his beer and take a seat in one of the chairs. "Tomorrow morning would've been plenty soon enough," I say, more than a hint of sarcasm in my voice.

Tony takes a swig of his beer, his expression serious. "Couldn't wait 'til then."

"What's up?" I ask, my bad temper instantly forgotten, my senses on alert at Tony's sombre tone.

"Your message said you picked up a woman outside Stanislaus, claiming that Lev Sarado is her father?"

"Kaylee Kemp," I nod. "Believe me, no one was more surprised than I was to see her again." I left a message for Tony at the station earlier, knowing that his partner, Daryl Jacobs, was fundamental in bringing down Lev Sarado. I hadn't expected Tony to hightail it over here at this hour, though, and the fact that he has increases the uneasy feeling in my gut.

"You know her?" Tony's eyebrows almost disappear into his blond hairline.

"We went to the same high school In Bakersfield. My family moved here with Dad's new job not long after I graduated, and I haven't seen her since."

"Well, I'll be damned! What are the fucking chances?" Tony exclaims. "So, she knows Lev is her real father?"

I nod again. "She's known for about a month. She found out when she lost her adoptive parents in a car wreck."

"Shit!" Tony explodes, sitting forward to place his beer on the coffee table in front of the sofa and rubbing his hands tiredly over his face.

"What's going on, Tony?"

Tony takes another swig of beer before answering. "During his investigation, Daryl discovered that Lev had an affair with a woman called Maria Campbell during his time UC. Turns out, she was the wife of the man Lev was tasked to bring down. It seems Maria broke things off with Lev and disappeared, just left everything behind. About six months later she gave birth to a baby girl and not long after that she was dead, shot by her husband, who managed to track her down." Tony explains. "The only reason Daryl knew Maria had a child was because she declared Lev as the father on the birth certificate, using his Russian family name of Ivanovich."

"Does Lev know?" I ask.

"No. Lev has no idea he has a daughter."

"Shit!" I say, echoing Tony's earlier curse.

"Until now, only a handful of people knew about Kaylee," Tony continues. "That's the way Daryl wanted it, for her own protection."

I sigh, knowing where Tony is going with this. "A man like Lev didn't get where he was without making a few enemies. If any one of them got wind of the fact that he has a daughter…"

Tony's expression is grim. "Exactly. Talking of, where is she?"

"I'm right here."

Both our heads whip around to find Kaylee standing at the foot of the stairs and my heart aches at the pain etched on her face, the sheen of tears in her eyes.

I rise from the sofa, moving toward her. "Kaylee…"

She holds up a hand, effectively stopping me in my tracks. "So, my real mother is dead then?"
☐

Kaylee

After my passionate encounter with Dawson on
the sofa, I escape upstairs, trying to gather my
thoughts and get my throbbing body back under
control. The passion that exploded between us
has knocked me sideways, the feeling of
Dawson's mouth on my skin making me feel
things I've never came close to before. If a
relatively innocent liaison with Dawson can make
me feel like this, I'm starting to think that the
other cheerleaders weren't exaggerating with
their whispered conversations about their
amazing sex lives, despite my experience being
to the contrary.

I hear Dawson's deep timbre as he talks with the
man who interrupted us - someone Dawson
obviously knows - and decide I may as well go to
bed.

As I start to shut the bedroom door, I hear
Dawson say my name, and curiosity gets the
better of me. I creep to the top of the stairs,

listening intently as pieces of conversation drift up toward me. Still not able to make anything out, I descend lower, praying the stairs don't creak under my feet.

"...investigation..."

"...Maria Campbell..."

"...shot by her husband..."

"...Lev has no idea he has a daughter..."

My hand flies to my mouth as I listen. My real mother is dead? And my real father has no idea I even exist! Which would explain why neither of them had ever tried to find me. Tough to do when you're either dead or in prison.

I'm not expecting the pain that hits me, knowing that I'll never get to meet my birth mother and that the chances of ever seeing my birth father are practically non-existent. I'll never know which characteristics I've inherited from them. Do I have my mother's eyes? My father's temper? There are massive holes in my history, in me, that I won't ever be able to fill.

"... talking of, where is she...?"

I'm brought back to the present, having unknowingly reached the bottom of the stairs.

"I'm right here," I say, feeling strangely removed from the whole situation.

Both men's heads whip around in surprise.

"Kaylee…" Dawson moves toward me, the sympathy on his face almost making me break down.

I hold up a hand and something about my expression stops him mid-stride. I feel so brittle that If he touches me now, I know I'll shatter into a million pieces. A new reality is carving itself out around me and it's taking everything I have to keep up.

"So, my real mother is dead then?" My words seem to hang in the air as Dawson and the other man exchange concerned looks.

Dawson is the first to break the silence. "I'm so sorry, Kaylee."

He moves toward me again and this time I don't stop him, letting him take my cold hand in his warm one. I make no objection as he draws me toward the sofa, so I can sink into its depths on wobbly legs. He takes a seat next to me, close enough that I can feel the comforting heat of his body.

"I'm Tony Cooper," the other man says, stepping forward and holding his hand out to me. I return his handshake with a firmness that belies how shaky I'm feeling. He looks to be in his late thirties, tall with blonde hair and a ruggedly handsome face with laughter lines around his eyes that suggest he's usually quick to smile. "I'm sorry I'm not introducing myself under better circumstances," he continues, his eyes conveying a genuine warmth.

I nod. "Me too. "Looks like I've put the cat among the pigeons coming here." I say, referring to the conversation I just overheard.

"Not your fault," Tony reassures me, folding his tall form into the chair next to the sofa. "I think this was inevitable. The truth has a way of coming out eventually," he says, and I know he's trying to make me feel better at the shit-storm I've unleashed with my presence here.

"I was so focused on getting answers as to why my birth parents didn't want me that it never even occurred me that Lev knew nothing about me." To my embarrassment, my voice breaks, and I bite my lip, struggling to regain my composure.

Dawson slips an arm around me, pulling me closer to his hard body and I sink gratefully against his already familiar warmth.

"Does anyone else know you're here?" Tony asks.

"No. Like I said, coming here was a spur-of-the-moment thing," I reply, and Tony casts a questioning look at Dawson.

"We came straight back here after I dropped the cruiser off at the station," Dawson says. "I didn't give despatch any information once I picked Kaylee up from the prison, just advised them that the situation was dealt with."

Tony looks relieved. "That's something, at least. The less people who know you're here, the better. It's good that you're staying here. You're in good hands with Dawson."

I can feel the heat climbing into my cheeks as I think about being in Dawson's hands again, in his bed, while he kisses my...

The sound of Tony's phone ringing makes me jump, tearing me from my wayward thoughts.

He pulls the phone from his pocket, glancing at the caller ID. "Sorry. I need to take this," he says, rising from the chair and walking into the kitchen. He closes the door behind him, leaving Dawson and I alone.

"How you holding up?" he asks, breaking the silence.

I release a shaky breath and look up at him. "I feel numb. It's just so much to process on top of everything else. It's not every day you find out your murdering father didn't know you existed and your birth mother is dead."

Dawson sighs, heavily. "We both know what it's like to lose a parent," he says, reaching out to pick up a strand of my hair between his fingers. "The murdering father part I can only imagine."

"I just wish I'd had the chance to meet her, you know? Ask her why she did what she did," I say, sadly. "Despite the shock of learning about my parentage, for the last month I've held onto the fact that there are still two people in this world I'm biologically connected to. There was a glimmer of hope that one day I'd get to meet my birth parents, fill in the blanks. Seems unlikely now."

Dawson pulls me toward him, wrapping his arms around me and I bury my face against his chest, inhaling the scent that is uniquely him, a scent that's already burrowing its way into my heart. I pull back, looking into his warm brown eyes.

"Um...Dawson? About earlier..."

The sound of the kitchen door opening cuts me off as Tony emerges, looking grim. If he notices how closely Dawson and I are to each other, he doesn't mention it.

"That was Daryl. He's in Bakersfield. Popular place, huh?" Tony says, seeing my look of surprise. "His fiancée's daughter lives there, and they haven't been able to get hold of her for more than twenty-four hours, so they drove down there to check on her."

"Seems a long way to drive after only twenty-four hours," Dawson says, echoing my own thoughts.

"It's...complicated," Tony replies, obviously not about to divulge any more than that. He sighs, rubbing a hand through his hair in agitation. "Just over an hour ago, Prue was attacked and stabbed outside her boyfriend's apartment."

I feel the color drain from my face at Tony's words. It's such an unusual name, but surely it can't be...?

"Prue? Is her boyfriend called Jake, by any chance?" My voice cracks on the question.

Tony's looks surprised. "You know her...?"

"Oh, my God! Is she dead?" I'm not aware of leaping to my feet until I'm standing in front of Tony, my eyes pleading with him.

I feel Dawson come to stand behind me and I turn to face him, grabbing his arms to hold me up as my legs turn to rubber. "She can't be dead,

Dawson, not her too! I can't...I only saw her a few hours ago!" I can hear the hysteria in my voice and I'm having trouble catching my breath.

"Kaylee, calm down," Tony says, firmly. "She's not dead. They've taken her to the hospital…"

I can't seem to absorb Tony's words, and everything is taking on a surreal feeling, the room shifting and tilting around me as my mind tries and fails to deal with the onslaught of emotion.

I feel like I'm suffocating, completely overwhelmed, short-circuiting like an overloaded outlet. My legs give way completely and the last thing I remember is Dawson calling my name.

DAWSON

I jerk awake as Kaylee moans, her body
thrashing against the bedclothes as if she's
caught up in a bad dream. I leave the chair I was
dozing in and climb onto the bed, pulling her
against me.

"Shhh. It's okay, sweetheart." I stroke her hair
back from her flushed face and her eyes flicker
open. Confusion clouds her blue gaze as she
tries to remember where she is.

"What happened?"

"You passed out." I smooth my hands
involuntarily up and down her back through the
bedclothes.

"Well, that's a first." she grimaces. "Tony…?"

"Is gone. Once he was sure you weren't dead," I
smile.

Kaylee gives me a weak smile in return, but it's quickly replaced by panic and she sits bolt upright. "Prue!"

"She's still in surgery. I've asked Tony to let me know as soon as he hears anything," I reassure her.

"I just can't believe it!" she whispers. "I mean, who would want to hurt her?" She drops her gaze to her lap, nervously twisting her fingers together. "I only met her yesterday for the first time and the way I behaved is...not something I'm proud of."

"Wanna tell me about it?" I ask, placing a finger under her chin and tilting her face up to mine when she doesn't answer. "No judgments, Kaylee."

She looks at me for a minute, then sighs as she comes to a decision. "I went to Jake's apartment yesterday afternoon. I heard that he'd been obsessing over a woman and I wanted to see what the competition looked like."

"Competition?"

"Yeah," she grimaces. "I told you earlier how I've been throwing myself into the party scene with a vengeance since I lost Mom and Dad. Well, there was one party, a few weeks ago, when I made a drunken pass at Jake Matthews, one of the Cubs players. I'm not proud of it but I was wasted and feeling all kinds of hurt and angry at the world. I was mortified when he turned me down and I...got upset."

I feel an unexpected surge of jealousy at the thought of Kaylee hitting on Jake, feeling conflicted that he could turn down a beautiful woman like her, but strangely relieved that he did.

"Despite his rejection, Jake was really kind to me. I think he saw through my alcohol-fuelled actions to the pain underneath and he took me to one side, told me that whatever I was going through, throwing myself at him or any other man wasn't the way to deal with it. He put my drunken ass into a cab, even paid the fare to make sure I got home safely."

My respect for the other man suddenly increases, knowing that he didn't take advantage of Kaylee when she was at her most vulnerable.

"So, why did you go to his apartment?" I ask, curiously.

"Because I'm a bad person," Kaylee says, a tear sliding silently down her cheek. "I mistook his kindness and compassion for something more. I think I was craving the way he made me feel that night, like someone still cared for me, and I set out to get his attention again, flirting with the other players, trying to make him jealous. Turning up at his apartment was a last-ditch attempt to get him to notice me. I knew Prue was there on her own, because I waited until I saw Jake leave. I had every intention of warning her off, but she wiped the floor with me and it was no less than I deserved. She gave me as good as she got," Kaylee says, with reluctant admiration. "So, there you go. Now you know what a horrible person I really am. How desperate I was for even a few crumbs of affection from someone."

"You're not a bad person, Kaylee. You've just been hurting. We all make mistakes when we're hurting. My dad always used to say you can only go forward by making mistakes. I remember him saying it to me when…" I stop, knowing this isn't the time or place to start sharing my own shit.

Kaylee raises an eyebrow in silent question, inviting me to continue. "No judgements, Dawson," she says, and I smile as she uses my own words against me.

"When I first joined the force, I got involved with one of the other recruits. Sherry and I went through our initial training together and we hit it off straight away. We started dating and things were going good. Then, after a few months, everything changed, she changed."

"How?" Kaylee asks, her brow furrowed.

"Sherry was always...highly strung, but I noticed her behaviour was becoming more erratic. Her moods would flip on a dime, she'd go from happy, to depressed, to angry in a heartbeat. It didn't matter what I did or didn't do, what I said or didn't say, nothing seemed to help. I was never sure which version of Sherry I was going to get. Things carried on like that for a while longer until I finally convinced her to get help. She agreed to see a psychiatrist, who did various tests and diagnosed her as bi-polar."

Kaylee's hand flies to her mouth. "Oh, Dawson…!"

I lift my hand, stalling her sympathy. "We broke up a few days later." I watch Kaylee's eyes widen with shock and anticipate the question in them.

"You want to know why didn't I stay with her."

"Yes," Kaylee says, her eyes holding mine unflinchingly. "Because, as I have good reason to know, you're not the kind of person who walks away from people in their time of need."

Her faith in me is humbling and it's all I can do to stop myself from hauling her across my lap and kissing her breathless. "I would have stayed with her, but she knew I wasn't in love with her. To be honest, I think she knew she wasn't in love with me either. We had similar interests, but it wasn't enough. The cracks were already starting to show in our relationship before she got ill, but she knew I would stay, that I wouldn't leave her to face things on her own. So, she was brave enough to make the decision for both of us. I've never quite forgiven myself for that, for not being stronger, fighting harder, doing the right thing."

"The right thing for who, Dawson?" Kaylee asks. "For you or for Sherry? It seems to me that you respected her wishes, allowed her to keep her pride intact. People think it's harder to stay in a relationship that's not working anymore, but sometimes the tougher choice is to walk away."

Kaylee's words make a lot of sense. I've carried a burden of guilt around since Sherry and I broke up because I couldn't give her what she needed, couldn't love her like she deserved.

"I think I know that, deep down, but it's hard not to blame yourself in that kind of situation," I say. "I hear from her periodically, and she's doing well. She left the force and moved back to Washington, where she's from. The docs have stabilised her medication and she's in a new relationship, so I guess it all worked out like it was meant to."

"We can't always see it at the time, though," Kaylee murmurs, and I'm sure she's talking about her own situation as much as mine.

"You're a good listener. I've never shared that with anyone other than my dad."

"Just returning the favor," she smiles. "You're a great listener yourself and you've already helped me more that you know."

"Anytime." I smile as she tries to hide a yawn. "You're out on your feet. I'll let you get some sleep," I say, climbing off the bed. "Call me if you need anything, I'm just down the hall."

I watch as she snuggles down and closes her eyes with a sigh before turning to leave the room.

"Dawson?"

I turn back toward her. "Yeah?"

"Thank you. For helping me, I mean. And for letting me stay here."

"You're welcome. Sleep well."

"You, too."

I close the door behind me, under no illusions that I'll get any sleep tonight.

I'm right, and after a restless night, I grab a quick shower, throw on a clean t-shirt with my jeans and head downstairs.

I grab my cell phone from the coffee table where I left it last night, seeing I have a missed call from Tony. I dial his number, walking into the kitchen and switching on the coffee machine.

"How is she?" Tony asks, answering on the second ring.

"Holding up. She's tough."

"Glad to hear it," Tony says. "I've got a few things I need to do first, but I'll swing by in about an hour. There's something I need to discuss with Kaylee."

"Like what?" I ask, my hackles instantly going up.

"Easy, champ. Just an idea I want to run by her," Tony replies.

"Let's just get one thing perfectly clear, Tony. Whatever this idea is, there's no fucking way that I'm letting you or anyone else put Kaylee through any more than she's already been through. She's still dealing with the news that her birth mother is dead, let alone the loss of her adoptive parents," I state, my tone leaving no room for argument.

"No one has any intention of making her do anything she doesn't want to," Tony says, and it seems an odd choice of words. "I'm not fucking stupid, Dawson, I know what I interrupted when I knocked on your door last night, and the way you looked at her just confirmed it."

"You're imagining things again, old man."

"Uh, huh. You keep telling yourself that, lover boy. I'll see you later."

Tony ends the call before I have time for a comeback. What the hell does he mean, the way I looked at her? I'm attracted to her, sure, and I think the feeling is mutual, if our little encounter on the sofa last night is anything to go by.

Cursing Tony under my breath, I head to the kitchen to make pancakes.

"Mmmm, something smells delicious."

I turn to see Kaylee standing just inside the doorway, dressed in the tank top and sweatpants from last night.

"Hey, sleepyhead. Your timing is perfect. I hope you like pancakes," I grin, flipping the last of them onto the stack I've already put on the warming plate.

"I love them but I'm so hungry I'd eat cardboard right now." She laughs as her stomach rumbles loudly, as if on cue. "Can I do anything to help?"

"Nope, all done, Go, sit and I'll bring it through. Coffee?" I ask

"Black coffee would be amazing, thanks," she replies, turning back toward the dining area.

"My cooking resume is pretty limited. Pancakes and chilli are the only two things I can make without poisoning myself or anyone else," I admit, placing the plate of pancakes on the table where I've already laid two places. "Help yourself to chocolate or maple syrup," I add, indicating the bottles on the table.

I grab the two mugs of coffee from the kitchen, placing one in front of Kaylee before taking a seat myself. I look over, smiling as I see her tucking hungrily into three pancakes liberally doused with both maple and chocolate syrup.

"Oh, my God! These are so good!" she moans, around a huge mouthful and the sound makes my dick twitch in my jeans.

"When did you last eat?" I ask, trying to distract myself from the fact that Kaylee makes eating pancakes look like the most erotic thing in the world.

"Um, yesterday morning," she replies, shovelling in another mouthful.

"No wonder you nearly face-planted the floor last night." I swallow hard as her tongue darts out to lick a spot of chocolate syrup from the corner of her mouth. Holy shit, that's hot!

"Enjoying food like this is definitely one of the benefits of not being on the cheer squad anymore," Kaylee says, gloriously oblivious to the enormous hard-on I'm hiding under the table. "I can't remember the last time I had pancakes. I'm used to counting every single calorie I eat to stay at a certain weight. Give me a few weeks and I'll be the size of a house!" She grins adorably, looking excited at the prospect of all the things she's going to eat.

"You'll look even more perfect with a few extra pounds on you," I say, my mouth bypassing my brain as I voice my thoughts, and Kaylee flushes at the compliment.

"I think a few of those pounds are already settling on my hips," she groans. "Thank you for feeding me. The least I can do is clear up." She stands and starts to collect the dirty plates and mugs.

"We'll do it together. Twice as many hands makes light work. Or, something like that," I grin.

We clear up in companionable silence and I'm amazed at how comfortable and normal this all feels with Kaylee. I'm enjoying her being around far more than I should for a man who's used to his own space. She's only been here for one night and it's already going to feel empty when she leaves.

Kaylee stifles a yawn, leaning back against the countertop as I finish stacking the dishwasher. "Sorry, didn't sleep too well. Tired as I was, I tossed and turned for ages. I kept thinking about what happened to Prue. Has there been any news?" she asks, turning worried eyes to me.

I shake my head. "No more than we knew last night. Tony's coming by in a little while, so he may know more."

I see her dejected look, and it feels as natural as breathing to reach out and pull her against me. Despite her height, I'm still a good head taller than her and her blond head rests snugly under my chin as she slides her arms around my waist and up my back, returning my hug with a sigh.

"I lucked out having you come to the prison last night," she mumbles against my chest.

"I think it was me who lucked out," I murmur, noticing her shiver as my hands trace up and down her back. I tilt her chin up so she's looking at me. "Remember what I told you last night?"

"I...uh..."

I told you we weren't finished...not by a long shot. I meant it."

"You did?" she asks, breathlessly.

I nod. "I can't stop thinking about how your mouth felt when we kissed, how hot it was when I put my mouth on you here." I move my hand down and brush it over her breast, my thumb finding the hard peak through the material of her top.

Kaylee moans and bites her lip at the light touch and it's probably the sexiest thing I've ever seen. Everything she does is sexy. "Why does it feel so good when you touch me?" she asks, breathlessly, the blue of her eyes darkening with desire. If it seems like an odd question, I don't notice, caught up in the demands of my own body.

"I want to look at you, Kaylee. Will you let me put my mouth on you again like I did last night?" I move my hand to the hem of her tank top, pushing it up just a little so I can feel the softness of the skin underneath. Kaylee places her hand over mine, and for a moment, I think she's going to stop me. Instead, she takes a step back and peels the top over her head, leaving her upper body naked to my burning gaze.

My eyes greedily eat up the pink-tipped mounds she's revealed, her narrow waist and the defined muscles of her stomach from her rigorous training. Her nipples harden under my gaze and I groan, feeling my cock press painfully against the seam of my jeans.

In one swift movement, I'm on her, lifting her onto the worktop and pressing my hips between her thighs. The added height of the worktop brings her glorious tits within easy reach as I bend to draw one nipple into my mouth. She tastes as good as I remember as I sample the other, loving the sounds of her moans above me and the feel of her legs wrapping around my hips as she pulls me closer.

She threads her hands through my hair, holding me against her, jerking uncontrollably as I gently bite her nipples, the only sound our harsh breathing in the quiet of the kitchen. I nibble my way up her neck and claim her mouth in a searing kiss, our tongues tangling in a frenzy of need.

I cup her breasts, thumbing the hard nubs, and her head rolls back, her moan of need almost enough to make me cum all over myself. I lift her, letting her slide down my body until her feet touch the floor, my hands delving into the waistband of her sweatpants, cupping her rounded ass and pulling her against the steely hardness of my throbbing cock.

"I'm on fire for you!" I growl, nipping her neck.

The knock at the front door seems loud in the silence of the house.

"You have *got* to be fucking kidding me!" I explode.

I drop my forehead to hers before reluctantly releasing her and scooping her top from the floor in what feels like a replay of last night. She looks just as shaken as I am as she quickly slips it over her head.

I completely lost myself in her, where we were and the fact that Tony was on his way all forgotten the second I touched her. I take a deep breath, trying to calm myself and my frustrated dick, sure Tony won't appreciate me answering the door with an enormous boner.

I reach for Kaylee's hand, linking my fingers with hers and tugging her toward the living area. She takes a seat on the sofa, smoothing her hair down in a vain attempt to compose herself. Her cheeks are flushed, her lips swollen from our kisses and the sight of her like that almost brings me to my knees. Tony will only need to take one look at her to know what we've been up to.

Talking of…

The polite knock has now turned into a loud banging at the door. "Okay! Okay! Leave the hinges on!" I yell as I throw the door open.

"I'm sorry, did I interrupt something?" Tony smirks, taking in my ruffled hair and t-shirt.

"Asshole," I mutter under my breath, loud enough that he can hear.

"Tut, tut! Someone's in a bad mood! Maybe you need a few rounds in the ring with yours truly to work off some of that bad temper."

"Nothing would give me greater pleasure," I say, through gritted teeth, turning to walk back to the living room and leaving Tony to follow me. "Just name the time and place."

"How about the gym after we're done here? I can spare an hour this afternoon."

The offer to blow off some steam is tempting, but I can't leave Kaylee.

Tony sees my hesitation. "Kaylee can come too. I'm sure she'd love to watch me hit the shit out of you, wouldn't you Kaylee? How you doing, angel?" he adds, grinning at her.

Tony's easy charm allows him to get away with giving women pet-names that should earn him a kick in the nuts in this day and age.

As if to prove my point, Kaylee returns his grin. "I'm doing much better thanks, and I'd love to come watch, although I don't know the first thing about boxing."

"What's to know? I hit him," Tony points at me, "and he falls down."

"In your fucking dreams, cream puff," I retort.

"We'll see," Tony smirks.

"Can I get you something to drink? Coffee? Arsenic?" I ask, pleasantly.

I look at Kaylee who's laughing openly at the two of us and seeing her like that has me grinning back at her.

Tony glances between us with a knowing look which annoys the hell out of me.

"Thanks, but no thanks. I've already had about twelve cups of coffee that tasted like arsenic this morning."

"Is there any more news on Prue?" Kaylee asks Tony.

"Daryl called me on the way here. She came through surgery well," Tony replies, and Kaylee sighs with relief. "They had to repair a tear from the stab wound, but there was no major damage. And the surgeon anticipates she'll make a full recovery, with time and rest."

"I still can't believe it!" Kaylee says. "Did they catch whoever it was?

"Oh, they caught him!" Tony says, with a small smile. "Prue beat the living crap out of him. His face was a bloody pulp and he was unconscious on the ground when Daryl and Trish got there. It seems Prue's a force to be reckoned with when it comes to self-defence."

"Good for her!" Kaylee says, her voice full of admiration.

"Yeah, but here's the kicker," Tony says. "The guy that attacked Prue used to be one of Lev's men."

I hear Kaylee's intake of breath and drop down on the sofa next to her, not liking where this conversation is going at all. "You mean…"

"He was a part of Lev's organisation," Tony confirms. "Diego Martinez is a piece of shit with a penchant for young girls. His brother, Guillermo, who also worked for Lev, is no better. Suffice to say the world will be a much safer place with them both behind bars, particularly as they had their fingers in all kinds of other messed up shit."

"What kind of messed up shit?" I ask, although I'm not sure I want to know the answer.

"I'll come onto that," Tony promises, "but first, I'd like to ask Kaylee a question." He turns to face her, giving her his full attention. "You said you came here because you wanted to see Lev. Are you sure that's what you really want, Kaylee?"

"Yes," Kaylee answers, without hesitation.

"You do understand the kind of crimes he's been charged with, don't you? Manslaughter, importing and distributing illegal substances, assault with a lethal weapon, grievous bodily harm, to name just a few," Tony says, bluntly.

"I know. I did some research when I found out he was my birth father," she says, quietly.

"I'm sorry, angel, but I need you to understand what kind of man he is. He's a master at manipulation and learned everything he knows from being undercover in a narcotics operation. Those eight years UC changed him, and he spent the following fifteen years living a double life and building himself a small empire, founded on the back of drugs money. He's intelligent and charming, but he's also cold and ruthless."

"I'm so proud!" Kaylee's words are saturated in sarcasm.

"What was your plan, if I hadn't turned up last night?" I ask, curiously.

She shrugs. "I didn't really have one."

"Well, unfortunately for you, getting to see Lev isn't quite as simple as turning up at the prison gates and demanding to be let in," Tony says, curtly.

"Believe me, I know that now," Kaylee defends herself. "Today it seems like the dumbest plan ever, but yesterday I wasn't thinking rationally. I haven't been thinking rationally for the last month."

"Having access to a prisoner can be a long-winded process, full of bureaucratic bullshit," Tony continues, seemingly unaffected by Kaylee's words. "With someone like Lev, who has so many criminal convictions stacked against him, it could take months."

"Bureaucratic bullshit route it is then," Kaylee says, lifting her chin as she looks at Tony. "I know he's not a saint, far from it, but I'm his biological daughter, his flesh and blood. He's the only parent I have left, and I deserve the opportunity to meet him and he deserves the opportunity to know I exist, despite what he's done. I'll never get to meet my birth mother now, ask her the questions I wanted to ask and if I don't at least try with Lev, there will always be a part of me, of my story, that's...incomplete. If it takes filling out a hundred forms, or taking DNA tests, I will. If it means waiting months, I'll wait. But I will see him."

"I see." Tony leans back in the chair, sighing heavily. "Then, I guess I should be the one to take you."

"What?" Kaylee's eyes round in surprise.

"What the fuck, Tony?" I explode, leaping to my feet, feeling completely blindsided and more pissed than I've been for a long time.

Tony holds up a hand. "Calm down, Dawson."

"Calm down? Don't fucking tell me to calm down! What happened to making sure she keeps a low profile?"

"Dawson, please! Let him speak," Kaylee pleads, grabbing my hand and tugging me back toward the sofa.

I give Tony a death stare before reluctantly sitting back down and reaching for Kaylee's hand. I link my fingers through hers and pull her against me, needing to feel her warmth. She makes no objection, leaning into me with a relieved sigh and I'm beyond giving a fuck what Tony makes of our body language right now. "This better be fucking good!" I snarl.

Tony nods, perhaps understanding the reason for my anger more than I do. "I know, and I'll explain everything, if you'll give me the chance." he says. "I'm sorry I was so blunt before, angel," he continues, turning his gaze to Kaylee, "but I had to be sure you knew what you were potentially getting into."

"Which is what, exactly?" I demand.

Kaylee squeezes my hand in silent reassurance and I take a deep breath, trying to rein in my anger. This is Tony, I remind myself. Someone I've known for five years. Someone I would trust with my own life. Not only is he my friend, he's a great cop, and I respect him enough to hear him out.

"Daryl's been in discussions with Lev, trying to cut a deal. He's been authorised to offer Lev a reduced sentence in exchange for information," Tony says.

"What kind of information?" I ask.

"We need a name. Lev still holds a lot of power, despite where he is. He could bring down any number of organised crimes if he chose to talk, but there's only one we're trying to convince him to co-operate on right now," Tony says.

"Which is?" Kaylee asks.

"A child trafficking ring."

"Shit!" I explode, looking across at Kaylee. Her pale face is pale, all traces of the soft flush of passion from our earlier encounter wiped from her cheeks.

"Which answers the question you asked earlier, about the other messed up shit the Martinez brothers were involved in," Tony's voice is full of disgust. "If Lev knew about it, he turned a blind eye, but he still has valuable information we could use to shut the whole sordid thing down."

"I presume he's not playing ball?" Kaylee asks, her face pinched.

"No," Tony shakes his head, his mouth grim. "Daryl's tried every angle, even appealed to the former cop in him to do the right thing. But, we keep coming back to the same issue. Lev wants to know what's in it for Lev. Ten years off a life sentence ain't gonna cut it. We need a different incentive, something of value to him that we can offer in exchange."

"And now you have it," I scowl, putting two and two together and not liking the answer one little bit. "Lev gets to see his daughter in exchange for the information you need," I say through gritted teeth. "You're going to dangle Kaylee in front of him like a carrot. No fucking way, Tony! Who the hell…?"

"I'll do it."

I turn to look at Kaylee, speechless.

She gets to her feet, pacing in front of the sofa. "Can't you see, Dawson? What Tony's just told us makes it even more important for me to see Lev! If there's a chance, even the slightest one, that I can convince him to change his mind, I've got to try," she says, turning pleading eyes on me. "This isn't just about me anymore, this is about stopping those sick bastards from hurting people, hurting innocent children!" she chokes, tears spilling down her cheeks.

Seeing her cry cuts me in half and my anger seeps out through my feet. I stand, pulling her into my arms and holding her tightly, my anger replaced with a cold fear at the prospect of what she wants to do. How has this woman wormed her way under my skin so quickly? "You don't have to do this," I say, feeling helpless.

Tony leans forward in the chair, his face sombre as he rests his elbows on his knees, clasping his hands together. "Dawson's right. You don't have to do this. You can go back to Bakersfield, forget you were ever here. It's your call."

"I can't do that. There are...other reasons I don't want to leave just yet," she says, tipping her head back to look at me and warmth spreads through me at the message in her eyes.

"So, what happens now?" I glower at Tony.

"I need to get the paperwork done, which will take a few days," Tony says. "Daryl's likely to be in Bakersfield until at least the end of the week, so it'll be down to me to make this happen."

"Is it okay to stay here for a few more days?" Kaylee asks, turning to look at me. "I mean, I can get a hotel if it's a problem…"

"You're not going to a hotel," I say, firmly. "You're staying here, with me, where I can keep an eye on you."

"You make me sound like a five-year-old who needs babysitting," Kaylee says, eyes flashing, and I'm relieved to see some of her fighting spirit returning.

"Yeah, well, you better behave and do as I say, or I might just put you over my knee and spank you," I grin, watching the color wash over her cheeks at the images my words invoke. The thought of spanking her rounded ass is beyond tempting.

Tony clears his throat loudly, his eyes moving back and forth between us. "Don't mind me, you two." he smirks. "By the way, Dawson, you're with me in Daryl's absence."

Relief washes over me at Tony's words, knowing that it's his way of keeping me actively involved and able to support Kaylee both emotionally and professionally.

Tony reaches into his jacket pocket and pulls out a plastic wallet. "There's just one other thing. You did say you'd be prepared to take a DNA test earlier, angel, and I know damn well Lev is going to want more than a copy of your birth certificate as proof that he's your biological father, so I'm going to need a swab from the inside of your cheek."

I know Tony's only doing his job, but I still want to punch his fucking lights out right about now.

"Guess you're really looking forward to that sparring match now, eh, champ?" Tony grins. He looks across at me and the smile slips a little.

"More than you could possibly imagine," I promise.

KAYLEE

Less than an hour later, I'm sitting in the boxing gym, watching Tony and Dawson sparring.

I quickly changed into shorts and a t-shirt before we left the house, noticing that my car was parked out front on the way out. Someone obviously brought it back as Dawson had promised.

Dawson was quiet on the ride over and I guess he's still pissed at the events that have unfolded today. I know he's not happy about my visit to see Lev, but I know in my gut that it's the right thing to do. I'm still trying to wrap my head around it all, knowing that I'm going to meet my birth father in just a few days. In some ways, I'm glad it's happening so quickly so I have less time to stress about what could go wrong.

Pain and guilt hits me as I think of Mom and Dad wondering what they would think of all this. I'm at war with myself, half of me angry at them for keeping the truth from me all these years, while the other half understands that they were probably just trying to protect me.

"Goddammit, Dawson! I'm sorry, okay?"

Tony's shout brings me out of my thoughts and back to the present. If I thought the two men were going to go easy on each other because of their friendship, I was very wrong. Dawson is channelling his earlier anger in Tony's direction, as he lands punch after punch on the older man. Tony's a fit guy, tall and muscular, but he's no match for Dawson. Not today.

I saw many a buff football player during my time as a cheerleader, but none of them come close to the perfection that is Dawson. I haven't been able to take my eyes off him for the last half hour, loving the way he moves, the flex of his muscles as he ducks and punches and how light he is on his feet, despite his height.

Our kiss in the kitchen earlier has only increased my attraction to him and it seems like the second he puts his hands on me I turn to mush. What I'm starting to feel for him is a million miles away from what I thought I felt for Jake.

The gym is busy; a large warehouse style building with high windows and old-fashioned fans on the ceilings, their heavy blades uselessly spinning the dense air. There are another four boxing rings besides the one Tony and Dawson are sparring in, all of which are in use, as well as heavy bags and various other sports equipment. The place is full of the smell of sweat and the grunts of men sparring fills the air.

Both Dawson and Tony are sweating and breathing heavily, their faces partially obscured by their protective headgear as they move around the ring, their movements almost like a dance. Suddenly, Dawson lets loose an almighty punch and Tony goes down, cursing and spitting out blood.

I leap up from the bench, instinctively grabbing the ropes and sliding into the ring like I'm some kind of WWE Diva. "You okay, Tony?" I ask, worriedly, bending down to check him over.

Tony rolls into a sitting position, blood trickling from his bottom lip as he smirks up at Dawson while I fuss over him. "I'm fine."

Dawson reaches down and pulls Tony to his feet. "You're getting slow, old man."

"Yeah, yeah. I let you have that one, champ. Feeling better now you've knocked me on my ass?"

"Much better," Dawson grins, slapping the other man on the back a little too hard. "Thanks for the warm-up."

Tony rolls his eyes. "I'm outta here. He's all yours, angel," he says, ducking under the ropes and heading toward the changing rooms.

I turn to look at Dawson, who's now taken off his headgear, his dark hair plastered to his forehead, his muscles slick with sweat. "Your turn," he says, crooking his finger at me.

I back up. "Oh, no! Not a chance, *champ*."

"Come on, *angel*, show me what you got."

"You really want me to show you what I've got?"

"I do." Dawson's eyes roam up and down my body, setting off sparks along the way and I resist the urge to throw myself at him.

"Okay. You asked for it." I walk to the corner of the ring and turn my back to him, allowing myself a little smile at his confused expression. Taking a deep breath, I launch myself into a back flip, landing it clean and pivoting into a high kick which misses Dawson's face by an inch, before dropping into a front splits at his feet. I look up to see Dawson gaping down at me and can't help the giggle that bubbles up from my throat.

"Wow! Not quite what I meant but that was...very enjoyable. Especially the splits part at the end," he grins, waggling his eyebrows.

I ignore his suggestive tone, jumping to my feet and giving him a bow. "Why, thank you, sir."

Dawson takes off his gloves. "Ready to learn some punches now?"

"Bring it on." I grin.

Dawson spends the next hour teaching me the basic punches; jab, hook, cross and upper cut, as well as how to duck and weave to avoid taking hits from an opponent.

"Tuck your thumb in," Dawson says, as I throw a cross punch. "Here, like this." He takes my hand in his, curling my fingers under and tucking my thumb against the knuckles of my index and second fingers. "Now, throw your punch and squeeze your fist as you strike your imaginary opponent."

I do as Dawson says, and he watches me a few times before coming to stand in front of me, holding his hands up, palms facing me as he gives me a target to aim for.

"Use your hips, that's where all your power is," he instructs, moving to stand behind me and resting his hands on my hips. "Now, throw your punch," he says, his breath stirring the hair against my neck and making me shiver. His nearness, along with his hands on me, is doing bad things to my concentration and my punch is sloppy compared to my previous efforts.

"Again." Dawson grabs my hips firmly, rotating them as I throw my punch. "Feel the difference?"

"Um, yeah." I clear my throat as the heat from his touch threatens to burn me up.

Yep, definitely feeling the difference.

Dawson's fingers bite into my hips for a second before sliding around and across my stomach, leaving a trail of fire behind as he pulls me against him so that I can feel his erection pressing against my butt. I'm breathing hard, but not from the boxing, his proximity playing havoc with my body.

A loud noise from the other side of the gym makes me jump, startling me from the sensual spell Dawson always seems to weave around me.

"I think we should probably call it a day." Dawson releases me and moves away, leaving me feeling empty. "I'll go grab a quick shower and we'll get going." His voice is husky as he turns away and I know he's just as affected as I am by whatever this is between us.

I'm falling fast, and it scares me like nothing else ever has.

DAWSON

I can feel the sexual tension stretching between us as we head home, so attuned to Kaylee now that our proximity in the car is doing crazy things to my body.

I pull up outside the house, cutting the engine and turning to look at her, taking in the natural color that the physical exercise has brought back to her cheeks. "You're determined to see this thing through with Lev, aren't you?"

"I've got to, Dawson, especially after what Tony told us today."

I feel uneasy about the whole thing. "For what it's worth, I don't want you to do it."

"I know," Kaylee sighs, "but I can't just turn my back on this, not now. And not just because of Lev, but because..." she stops, her gaze dropping to her hands as she twists them nervously in her lap.

I cup her chin, tilting her head toward me. "Because of what, Kaylee?"

"Because of you," she whispers, lifting her eyes to mine, "because of how you make me feel."

It takes me a full minute to absorb what she's saying and by the time I do, her cheeks are flaming with embarrassment. "I'm sorry, I didn't mean to…" Her eyes widen with surprise as I open my car door and climb out. "Dawson…?"

I can see the uncertain look on her face as I stride around the car to open her door, ignoring her protests as I pull her out of her seat and throw her over my shoulder. I manage to get the front door open, hardly slowing down to kick it shut with my foot before carrying her upstairs, lowering her into the middle of my super-kingsize bed.

"I thought you were running away for a minute there," she says breathlessly.

"Not a fucking chance," I promise. "I just want you on a bed where I can enjoy you, not some rushed encounter on the back seat of my car."

A strange look passes over her face, but it's gone so quickly, I'm sure I imagined it.

I sit on the bed, tugging her toward me so she's straddling my thighs. Even through two layers of clothing, the heat of her pussy pressing against me has my cock pulsing with need.

"Kiss me, Dawson," Kaylee moans, threading her hands through my hair and pulling my head to hers. Our mouths collide, and I groan as Kaylee's tongue steals into my mouth, tangling with mine in a rhythm that's matched by her hips as she moves restlessly against me.

I tear my mouth from hers, sliding my hands down to the hem of her t-shirt and she raises her arms so I can remove it. I unclip the lacy bra she's wearing underneath, peeling the straps down her arms as I slowly reveal her luscious tits with their pink tipped crests. Trailing my lips down her throat, I cup her breasts, pulling a nipple into my mouth, suckling first one and then the other, lavishing them with my tongue.

"Dawson, that feels so good!" Kaylee gasps, her back arching to prolong the contact.

The sound of my name on her lips unleashes the beast within me and I gently bite down on a nipple, causing her to cry out again. Her breathy moans make my cock strain painfully against my jeans and I know I'm not going to be able to hold back much longer.

I press her back into the bed and stand, quickly divesting myself of my clothes. Kaylee's eyes drink me in, landing on the inked skin across my chest and abs before rounding at the sight of my impressive shaft standing rigidly away from my body. If possible, the feel of her eyes on me makes me swell even more, pre-cum glistening on the end of my throbbing cock.

I lean over and hook my fingers into the waistband of her shorts pulling them smoothly down her long legs, along with her panties. This time, it's my eyes that widen as I take in her smooth, bare pussy. I look up to see the flush crawling up her neck and into her cheeks as she sees the question in my eyes.

"It's just easier when you're in revealing clothing all the time," she says, self-consciously.

I still her hands as she tries to cover herself, wanting to see every exquisite inch of her. "Believe me, I'm not complaining," I growl. It's the most erotic thing, seeing the dampness that coats her pussy, my cock pulsing even harder at the visible sign of her desire.

I settle my mouth just above her bare mound, making her gasp as I tease and nibble my way over the smooth skin of her stomach, my teeth nipping at her sensitive flesh.

"Please, Dawson!" Kaylee moans, squirming under my touch as her hands reach for me.

The last of my control shatters with her breathy plea and I promise myself that I'll be back to savour the sweetness of her pussy, but right now, I need to be inside her. I reach into the bedside drawer for the foil packet, tearing it open with my teeth and sheathing myself with trembling hands before settling my hips between her thighs.

"I'm big, baby, so I'll try to go slow. I want you to tell me if you need me to stop, okay?"

Kaylee nods, and I capture her mouth in a soft kiss, cherishing her lips as I try to calm my body a little. I probe her entrance, giving her the first inch of me, trying to stretch her tight channel as I ease a little further inside her. I withdraw and press in again, deeper this time, and holy fuck, it feels amazing! She's incredibly tight and the sensation is beyond anything I've ever felt.

I grit my teeth, trying to hold onto my promise to go slow, but when Kaylee moves underneath me, lifting her hips a little to accommodate me, I can't hold back any longer and with one powerful thrust, I submerge myself balls-deep in her delicious heat.

"Dear God, Kaylee!" I choke, barely aware of her whimper as pull back and thrust inside her again.

My orgasm is upon me within seconds and I desperately try to put on the brakes, wanting it to last, to give her pleasure too, but it's no use and with a hoarse cry, I'm cumming hard and fast, unable to stem the flow of my seed as my body strains against her with the intensity of my climax.

I collapse on top of her, trying to catch my breath as I come down from one of the most amazing releases I've ever had. Still breathing heavily, I look up at a wide-eyed Kaylee.

"Are you okay?" she asks, looking genuinely worried. "You looked like you were dying."

A little alarm bell goes off at her expression. "I'm fine, baby. More than fine. Fucking amazing!" I reassure her. "Apart from the fact that I wanted you so bad I came in about ten seconds flat. That's never happened to me before. I'm sorry, I just couldn't stop." I kiss her softly, still shaking from the force of the pleasure she's just given me.

I'm suddenly aware that most of my weight is resting on her soft body and I roll away, swinging my legs out of the bed and heading to the bathroom to quickly clean up, wanting nothing more than to get back to her warm body and finish what we've just started.

I walk back into the bedroom, coming to a halt when I find Kaylee already out of bed, pulling her shorts on over her panties, her upper body still bare. I lean against the door frame, crossing my arms in front of my chest. "Where do you think you're going?"

"Um...back to my room?" She crosses her own arms self-consciously over her chest.

"Your room? Why?" Her behavior is...odd. Something's not adding up here.

"Because the sex is over," she says, matter-of-factly.

"Who said it was over? I'm nowhere near done with you!" I promise, pushing away from the door frame and walking toward her.
Kaylee frowns. "But you...you know, had an...um…"

"What? An orgasm? Yeah, I did, and it was fucking amazing!" I say bluntly. "But you didn't, and that's my fault but...wait a minute..." A chilling thought suddenly occurs to me. "Kaylee, please tell me you've had sex before!"

"Yes, Dawson, I've had sex before!" she snaps, her cheeks flaming as she wraps her hands more tightly across her breasts. "Once," she mumbles, reluctantly.

My mouth drops open as I try to grasp the fact that the drop-dead, gorgeous woman in front of me has only ever had sex once! Well, technically, twice now. Remorse follows hot on the heels of my shock and I close my eyes, remembering how worked up I was, how I lost control, her whimper as I lost myself in her body. Oh, God, I hurt her!

I open my eyes, seeing the pain in Kaylee's expression as she obviously misunderstands my look of regret.

"Kaylee…"

"It's okay, Dawson." She shakes her head, a tear escaping down her cheek as she turns for the door.

"Oh, no you don't!" I'm in front of her in a flash, ignoring her squeal as I throw her over my shoulder for a second time and stalk back to the bed. "You're not going anywhere!"

KAYLEE

"Put me down!"

Dawson drops me unceremoniously in the middle of the bed and I glare at him, my temper flaring at his high-handedness.

I pull myself into a sitting position, grabbing the sheet to cover my breasts and wrapping my arms around my knees as I fight tears. Things had started out so well and I'd wanted Dawson so badly, experiencing sensations I didn't know were possible as he touched me, kissed me. My body had come alive and I'd never wanted it to end. But it had, all too quickly. Just like before.

My eyes linger on the play of muscles in Dawson's shoulders and arms as he quickly pulls on his jeans, coming to sit on the edge of the bed and raking an agitated hand through his hair. The tattoos on his chest and lower abs give him a slightly dangerous look and my fingers itch to trace them. He's the perfect specimen of a man and the sight of him takes my breath away, even now.

"Kaylee, if I'd had any idea how inexperienced you are…"

"What? You wouldn't have had sex with me?" I ask, bitterly. "I'm pretty sure that was regret I just saw on your face, Dawson!"

"Because I lost control, not because I regret having sex with you! I've never wanted anyone the way I want you, Kaylee," Dawson admits. "The second I touch you, I lose my head. I've never felt anything like that, not with anyone! If I'd known you were practically a virgin, I would've taken more time with you. A *lot* more time," he emphasises.

"Why?" I glare at him. "What difference would that make?"

Dawson looks at me like he can't quite believe what I'm asking. "All the difference in the world, sweetheart," he sighs, and the endearment makes my stomach flip. "Sex should be a pleasurable experience for both parties, but I didn't last long enough for you to have an orgasm. That's the regret you saw on my face before" he explains. "You do know it can be good for you too, right? You've had an orgasm before?"

The colour blooming in my cheeks gives me away and I shake my head. "I can't have one. The only time I had sex was on the backseat of a car and it was painful and I felt used afterward. It was over in seconds, we didn't even undress fully, just removed what was necessary." I drop my eyes to the bed in front of me. "Once he...you know...finished, he straightened his clothing and took me home. Meri, my best friend, said he was a selfish asshole and that it's probably not always like that, but..." I shrug, "...I don't know any different."

Dawson closes his eyes briefly, as if in pain. "When you say you can't have an orgasm..."

I feel my blush deepening, not quite sure how we got into such intimate territory - more intimate, in some ways, than sex itself. "I...uh...tried to...you know...touch myself in the past, but I guess I wasn't relaxed enough or I wasn't sure what I was doing, what I was meant to be feeling. I just felt clumsy and nothing would happen. The closest I've come to that kind of feeling...is with you in the last few days," I admit. "Maybe I'm not normal and the problem is me. Maybe there's something wrong with me and my vagina doesn't work properly."

Dawson smiles at my choice of words. "There's absolutely nothing wrong with you or your vagina, Kaylee." He reaches out to tuck a strand of hair behind my ear and his smile grows as he sees me shiver. He moves closer, his hand smoothing over the bare skin of my arm, leaving a rash of goosebumps in its wake.

I look up at him as he dips his head toward me and our eyes lock, a now familiar warmth unfurling in my stomach and landing between my legs at the heat of that gaze. He brings his mouth to within an inch of mine and it's all I can do not to close the small distance and press my lips to his.

"When I touched you earlier, you went up in flames," he says softly. "I could see it, feel it. Your body reacted to me in way that blew my mind and my control," he whispers, his breath fanning over my lips which are still sensitive from our earlier kisses. "And now, I'm going to make it up to you, show you just how normal, how perfect, you are. How much pleasure your body is capable of."

I search his eyes for a long minute, wanting so badly to believe what he's saying, just as much as I've come to believe in him in such a short space of time.

My nod is almost imperceptible but it's all he needs, and my eyes flutter shut as he closes the inch between us, kissing me softly, almost reverently, pushing his hand through my hair to hold me to him. He flicks his tongue across my closed mouth, eliciting an involuntary moan which he takes advantage of as his tongue pushes inside my mouth.

"This is all about you now, Kaylee. Whatever you want, whatever you need, tell me and I'll give it to you," he murmurs against my lips.

I hear the sincerity of his words and feel the prickle of tears behind my eyes. Taking a deep breath, I release the sheet I'm still clutching to my chest, allowing it to slip down to my waist, watching as his eyes fall to my breasts. He swallows hard, but he doesn't make any move to touch me.

Reaching across, I run my fingers through his thick, dark hair, tracing my fingers along his forehead and down his jaw, loving the tickle of his soft beard against my fingertips. He places his hand over mine, kissing my palm without breaking eye contact and I feel the intensity of his gaze all the way to my core.

"Tell me what you want, sweetheart."

I trail my fingers lightly over my breasts. "Will you...put your mouth on me... here?"

"I thought you'd never ask!" he growls, and tugs me toward him so that I'm straddling him like before, my knees resting on either side of his hips, my chest on a perfect level for his mouth.

My breath hitches as he splays his hands across my back, his mouth hovering in front of me, the promise of his lips making me move instinctively against him. As his mouth settles over my nipple, heat shoots to my core and I can't help the gasp that escapes me. I tangle my fingers through his hair, holding him to me as he moves from one breast to the other until I'm squirming in his lap, my body yearning for more.

With one swift motion, Dawson flips us over so that I'm on my back and his mouth descends on mine in a kiss that makes my toes curl. I wrap my legs around his hips, my body seeking a closer contact with him. I'm aching, and I need him to make the ache go away.

"Slow down, baby," Dawson whispers, smoothing my hair back from my flushed cheeks as I writhe underneath him. "We've got all the time in the world. I'm going to make this so good for you. I don't ever want you to doubt the pleasure your body can give you again."

He moves down my body, nibbling his way down my neck to my breasts again, pressing them together with his hands so that he can sweep his tongue over both of my nipples. I cry out at the unbelievable sensation, my body straining mutely against him for more and he's only too happy to oblige as he trails his lips down my body, nipping and tasting me as he goes.

I tense as he begins to slide one hand inside my shorts and he pauses, looking up at me. "I want to touch you," he says. "I want you to feel what it's like to be loved, really loved."

I nod, trying to relax as he slides my shorts down my legs along with my panties, and for the second time in the space of an hour, I'm completely naked under his hungry eyes.

"You are exquisite," he says, his head dipping to the soft skin of my stomach as he nips me gently. My muscles clench at the delicious contact of his mouth as he trails kisses between my breasts and up my neck, before dipping his head to mine. He kisses me, slow and deep, our tongues tangling as his hand moves down, skimming over my breasts and along my hip before circling inward.

Before I realize what he's doing, his hand is sliding over my mound, his finger finding my moist cleft as he opens me up to his touch. I jerk at the unfamiliar contact, my tender flesh reacting to the invasion of his finger in such an intimate area.

"Am I the first man to touch you here, Kaylee?" Dawson asks, his voice gruff.

"Yes," I whisper.

"Shit!" Dawson says, resting his forehead against mine. "I feel about ten fucking feet tall!"

"Well, you kind of are...almost," I smile. My smile quickly turns to a gasp as he moves his hand on me, spreading my folds open even further as his finger finds the most sensitive part of me, the sensation almost lifting me off the bed. He does it again, and then again, until I can't help but move with him, encouraging the friction of his finger against me as a feeling unlike anything I've ever known starts to build in my body.

Without breaking the rhythm of his hand, Dawson dips his head to my breasts again, grazing my nipples with his teeth so that I'm gasping and squirming against him as the pleasure he's giving me intensifies.

"Dawson?" I gasp, a little frightened at the strength of the feeling that begins to bite into my body as his hand moves faster, becoming more demanding.

"Let go, baby," Dawson growls, nuzzling my neck as he slips one, then another, finger inside me. "This is what it feels like, Kaylee. I can feel you contracting around my fingers. You're going to cum. Your first orgasm and I get to see it, watch every second of it."

His words send me over an unknown edge and I hear myself cry out as if from a distance as my body spasms with the force of my first climax. I grind myself against Dawson's fingers, my body bowing off the bed as I try to hold onto a pleasure unlike anything I could ever have imagined.

Before I can come down from the high, Dawson slides down my body, pressing my thighs open with his hands and fastening his warm mouth on my hyper-sensitive flesh. I nearly come up of the bed again as his tongue finds my sensitive nub, sucking and licking me towards another orgasm.

"I can't!" I gasp, my head thrashing from side to side and my hands gripping the sheets at my hips as my body bucks against his mouth.

"You can, and you will, baby. Give me another," Dawson demands, and my body obeys, my mouth open in a silent scream as my body convulses again and again until every drop of pleasure is wrung from me and I collapse back onto the bed, utterly spent.

"Oh. My. Fucking. God!" I mumble, hardly able to find the energy to form words, my body completely boneless. I'm vaguely aware of Dawson pulling me against him and I snuggle into his warmth as I give in to sleep.

DAWSON

I quickly strip off my jeans before pulling Kaylee against me and covering us with the sheet. My heart melts as she snuggles into me and within seconds, she's asleep.

It seems impossible after such a short time, but my cock is on fire after watching Kaylee orgasm, not once but twice. I'm still coming to terms with what I've learned in the last hour and hope that the pleasure I've just given her goes some way to making up for earlier.

The idea that Kaylee is as innocent as she is floors me, especially with the way she looks. But that's just the wrapping - her warmth, intelligence and compassion are the real gift and I can't believe I'm lucky enough to be lying next to her, watching her sleep after watching her cum for the first time. Despite our rocky start this evening, my chest swells at the thought that I'm the only one who's ever seen her like that and the Neanderthal in me roars.

I pull her warm body even closer, the sound of her peaceful breathing washing over me as I close my eyes.

I wake a few hours later, glancing at the bedside clock to see it's gone seven in the evening. I'm lying on my back with Kaylee spread across my chest, one of her legs thrown over mine as she sleeps, and I can't help but smile at the adorable little snoring sounds she's making.

Without waking her, I gently disentangle myself and slide from the bed, pausing to look down possessively at her naked body relaxed in sleep.

She's mine.

The thought pops into my head and I know that it's what I want. For her to be mine, just like I'm hers. I know it now after the last few hours together. A part of me may have even known it five years ago, when Thursday evenings would be one of the highlights of my week because I got to see her, even if it was a purely innocent arrangement to get me through graduation.

The strength of the emotion I'm beginning to feel for her now freaks me the fuck out and, grabbing some clean clothes, I head to the bathroom for a cold shower. What if I fall for her and things go bad like they did with Sherry? I'm not sure I could recover from that with Kaylee. Not now. Not after what we've just shared.

I shut off the shower and quickly dry off, pulling on sweatpants and a clean t-shirt. Kaylee stirs as I move around the bedroom, rolling onto her back and stretching, giving me a very pleasant eyeful of her naked body. Her eyes open and she smiles sleepily as she sees me standing by the bed, blushing all the way from her perfect tits up to her face.

"Where do you think you're going? she murmurs. "I'm nowhere near done with you."

I smile as she repeats my earlier promise to her, sinking down on the edge of the bed and leaning over to claim her lips. Her arms snake up around my neck and, with a groan, I deepen the kiss as she opens her mouth under mine.

"You hungry?" I ask, nibbling her bottom lip.

"Starving," she replies, and I'm not entirely sure she's talking about food.

"Wanna order takeout for dinner?"

"Thai?" she says, hopefully.

"Thai, it is."

"Oh. My. God!" Kaylee groans, savouring the last mouthful of Thai green curry. "I'd forgotten how good that tastes!"

She looks utterly radiant, the blond hair curling around her face still damp from her shower earlier. Wondering if she's naked under the robe she's wearing has been driving me crazy for the last hour.

"I think you inhaled it," I grin at her across the dining table. "That was delicious. Good choice."

"I love Thai food. Haven't had it for over two years, but it was worth the wait." She looks at me, her blue eyes full of contentment. "Just like you were."

I push my chair back, moving around the table to pull her into my arms, loving the flush of color that stains her cheeks as I bend to kiss her.

Kaylee groans at the touch of my mouth against hers, winding her arms around my neck and deepening the kiss. "I don't think I'll ever get enough of you now," she says, pressing herself against me so that we're molded together from chest to thigh.

"Is Tony coming over tonight?" she asks, unexpectedly.

"No, why?" I ask, frowning.

"I just wanted to check we weren't going to have any interruptions. Tony seems to have a knack for it," she grins, looking up at me from under her lashes.

My heart rate picks up at her meaning. "Are you sure?" I ask, cupping her face in my hands and smoothing my thumbs across her cheeks.

"I've never been more certain about anything, Dawson. I want to experience it all, but only with you."

That's all the encouragement I need as I swing her up into my arms and carry her back to the bedroom, letting her body slide slowly down mine as I lower her to the floor.

I thread my hands through her hair, tipping her head back as my mouth finds hers, my tongue thrusting into her mouth in a rhythm that makes her groan. Our earlier intimacy has done nothing to cool my ardor for her and my swollen cock is already seeking the moist warmth of her body.

Her hands move to the hem of my t-shirt, sliding underneath and around my back, holding me to her as my mouth plunders hers. Not content, she pushes it up and I break the kiss, lifting my arms so she can pull it over my head. She sweeps her hands around my chest before trailing her fingers down over my abs, and my muscles clench involuntarily at the featherlight touch.

"I like the ink," she murmurs.

"I had them done after Dad died."

She traces the patterns on my chest. "Angel wings. Very apt." Leaning forward, she presses her lips to my chest, her mouth moving softly over the firm skin, tracing the tattoo with her tongue. I groan loudly when she flicks her tongue across my nipple, feeling it all the way down to my aching balls.

She pulls back to look at me. "I don't really know what I'm doing," she admits, "I just know I want to touch you, taste you. Is that...okay?"

"Sweetheart, whatever you do is more than okay. There's no wrong way to do this, so long as we both enjoy it. You could smear me in honey and dip me in cornflakes and it would be okay," I say, smiling as I lower my mouth to hers again, needing another taste of her sweet lips.

"If I did that I'd just want to eat you," Kaylee smiles against my mouth and the thought of her 'eating' me conjures up all kinds of images, making me groan again.

"Baby, I'll take great pleasure in teaching you how to eat me some time," I growl, backing her up until her knees hit the bottom of the bed.

She suddenly gets my meaning and laughter bubbles up from her throat. I love the sound, the way it lights up her face and makes her blue eyes sparkle.

My hands go to her waist, tugging at the ties of her robe and my breath catches when my earlier question is answered as it parts to reveal that she's naked underneath. I slide the robe down her shoulders so that it lands in a pool at her feet, stepping back a little as my eyes rake hungrily up and down her body, taking in her pert, full breasts and narrow waist and hips. I give her a gentle nudge and she topples backward on the bed, her hair spread out around her like a halo.

"I love the way you look at me," Kaylee moans, moving restlessly under the heat of my gaze. "You make me feel like I'm the only woman in the world."

"You are, to me," I say, softly, quickly divesting myself of my sweatpants so that I'm standing before her naked.

"You're…breathtaking," she whispers, and my cock swells even more as her rapt gaze skims up and down my body, drinking me in as I did with her moments ago. She swallows nervously as her eyes land on my throbbing shaft. "Is that...legal?"

I burst out laughing at her question, sinking down on the bed next to her and pulling her against me. "Legal, and all yours, sweetheart." I dip my head to hers and nibble at her lips. She opens her mouth, moaning as she meets the thrust of my tongue with her own.

She places her palms against my chest, gently pushing me so that I roll onto my back as she straddles my hips. I groan as she dips her head, licking and nibbling her way across my chest and down my abs, her mouth and tongue creating magic wherever they land.

"You're a fast learner," I rasp, as she grazes her teeth across my lower abs, making my cock jerk with need.

She sits back, looking like a goddess as she rests her weight on my thighs. Hesitantly, reaches forward to take my swollen length in her soft hands. "It feels like velvet," she says, wonderingly, and the sensation of her fingers moving on me has my hips lifting instinctively off the bed. "Show me what to do." Her eyes are full of the need to please me.

I groan, covering her hands with mine. "You need to stop, baby, or I'm not gonna last," I say, gently removing her hands and pulling myself into a sitting position with her still straddling me.

"I'm sorry, I didn't mean to..."

I silence her with a finger against her lips. "You didn't do a single, fucking thing to apologise for," I reassure her. "I just want us to take our time, and if you keep touching me like that, it'll be over far too quickly. I want this to be so good for you. I want to be deep inside you, looking into your eyes when you cum. But most of all. I want this to be special, the kind of first time you should've had."

Kaylee swipes at the tears that spill down her cheeks, leaning in to kiss me softly. Her hands cup my face as her thumbs smooth over my jaw, her touch conveying something far deeper than mere passion. Suddenly, I can't get close enough to her, wanting to fuse our bodies so tightly together that I don't know where I end, and she begins.

I flip her over so that she's underneath me, my body pressing hers into the mattress as our hungry mouths collide. I tear my mouth away, my lips burning a trail down her throat to her tits, pulling a taut nipple into my mouth as my thumb strokes the other, spurred on by the soft moans she makes as I graze the tight buds with my teeth.

My mouth continues its fiery trail down her body, gripping her hips with my hands as my tongue dips into her navel before moving lower, teasing over her bare mound. She gasps, and her thighs fall open, her body already anticipating the pleasure to come as my tongue slides between the swollen lips of her pussy. I groan at the taste of her sweet nectar, burying myself nose deep in her slick folds as I hone in on her clit.

"Dawson!" Kaylee cries out, her hands clawing at me as I swipe my tongue back and forth over her sensitive flesh. My mouth and lips envelop her as I suck and nibble at her, feeling her pussy start to quiver with the onset of her orgasm.

"Don't cum yet, baby," I say, moving back up her body to kiss her, giving her a taste of her own honey. "You're close, and I want to be inside you when it happens."

Her hands clutch at me and I can see the overwhelming need in her eyes. "Please,

Dawson!" she gasps, her hips moving beneath me.

"It's okay, sweetheart, I'm going to take care of you now."

I reach for a condom, but her hand stalls mine as I pull it from the drawer. "I'm on the pill. I trust you and I don't want anything between us."

Her words shatter what little control I have left, the thought of no barriers between us making my cock leak a little cum. I grab a pillow, sliding it under her hips as I nudge her legs open with mine and position myself at her entrance. I reach down, my thumb finding her clit again as I gently press my hips forward, letting her have the tip of me.

"You okay, baby?" I ask, through gritted teeth, desperately trying to hold onto some semblance of self-control.

"More than okay," she gasps. "I want all of you! Fill me up, Dawson. Please!" she begs.

"I will, baby, so deep!" I promise, keeping the pressure on her clit as I thrust forward, my passage easier this time as her pussy juices bathe my shaft. I pull back and thrust inside her again, hearing her mewl of pleasure as I bottom out inside her, so aroused that she accepts my full length easily.

I lift my hand to her mouth, pressing my thumb to her lips, watching as her tongue flicks out to taste her juices and it's one of the hottest things I've ever seen. Her legs clamp around my hips as she grinds herself against me, her body instinctively finding the position that gives her the friction she needs with each thrust of my hips.

"Dawson, it feels so good," Kaylee moans, throwing her head back and crying out with pleasure as I stroke in and out of her tight channel again and again. I can feel the beginnings of the contractions deep inside her as her climax builds and the sensation of my balls drawing up as my own orgasm fast approaches.

"Look at me!" I demand, and Kaylee's eyes fasten on mine as I move in and out of her welcoming body.

"I'm going to…Oh, God!" Her back bows off the bed as her orgasm slams into her, but she doesn't look away, her eyes holding mine, her pupils dilated, as the pleasure bites into her body.

Seeing her cum pushes me over the edge and with a final grunt, I'm cumming with her, crying out hoarsely as my cock pulses endlessly, emptying every last drop of my seed inside her in an orgasm that nearly makes me lose consciousness.

I collapse on top of her, trying to catch my breath in the aftermath, both our bodies slick with sweat.

"Oh, wow!" Kaylee says, still breathing heavily. "That was…"

"Ridiculously good," I laugh, rolling onto my back and pulling her against me, still trying to calm my breathing as I come down from the incredible high.

"I never knew it could be like that, feel like that," Kaylee murmurs, nuzzling her face into my neck.

"Neither did I," I admit.

Kaylee pulls back to look at me. "Really? But you've been with other women. Isn't it always like that?"

"I've only been with two other women besides Sherry and I can assure you I've never experienced anything close to what we just shared." I assure her.

"Never?" she asks, her eyes widening.

"Never." I repeat, holding her gaze so she can see the sincerity of my words.

"That makes me feel a little better because I wasn't sure if I felt grateful to those other women for your experience or so jealous I wanted to rip their throats out," she smiles wickedly.

I chuckle, placing a kiss on the end of her nose. "Steady on there, spitfire. You have nothing to be jealous of. Sex is...different with you."

"How?"

I sigh, my hand absently smoothing up and down her back as I try to find the right words. "It's...deeper, more profound."

"That's how it feels to me too. I can't imagine doing this with anyone but you, Dawson. I never dreamed how much pleasure I could feel."

"I think it's safe to say we've proven there's nothing wrong with your vagina," I grin. Kaylee blushes prettily. "Not where you're concerned. I'm pretty sure it wouldn't behave like that for anyone else!"

"It better not!" I growl, rolling her onto her back and pinning her underneath me, kissing her soundly. The thought of Kaylee being with another man makes me want to break things.

As if sensing my thoughts, Kaylee cups my face, looking into my eyes. "I don't want anyone but you, Dawson. I know it's only been a few days but…I'm already a little bit in love with you."

My heart threatens to pound out of my chest at her words, knowing how much courage it must have taken for her to admit that. I want to tell her I feel it too, and the words are on the tip of my tongue, but what if she's mistaking physical attraction for something more? She's still grieving, and she's never been in a relationship before, never experienced the kind of pleasure we've shared with anyone else. What if one day she wants to know what it's like to be with someone different? I'm not sure I'd be able to let her go. Not without my heart going with her.

"Kaylee, I…"

She places her fingers against my mouth, cutting off what I was going to say. "It's okay. I'm not expecting declarations of love in return," she says, her words conveying a depth of maturity beyond her years. "I can wait," she smiles.

I dip my head to hers, swallowing the ball of emotion in my throat as I kiss her softly, cherishing her mouth, trying to convey in actions what I'm not ready to put into words...yet.

"Um, Dawson?" Kaylee asks uncertainly, tearing her mouth from mine.

"Yeah, baby?" I mumble, trailing my lips down her neck.

"I seem to be leaking."

I pull back sharply to look at her before suddenly realising what it is she's feeling, and my shoulders start to shake with laughter.

"It's not funny!" she says, punching me on the arm and glaring at me.

"Oh, sweetheart! You are absolutely priceless!" I choke, resting my forehead against hers. "I came inside you, baby, and that's what you can feel. Laws of gravity. What goes up must come down."

"Oh! Right then, I better go...uh...clean up."

She wriggles out from underneath me and I can't resist giving her rounded ass a playful slap as she heads to the bathroom. I swear to God, she's just about perfect and the last few days with her have been amazing, despite the circumstances that brought her here and the thought of what still lies ahead. She's brought color to my life and everything feels brighter, more vivid when I'm with her.

She walks back into the bedroom, completely at ease with her nakedness now, and my feelings of possessiveness deepen as I look at her. She

climbs back into bed and I pull her to me,
wrapping her up against me, her contented sigh
echoing exactly how I'm feeling. I kiss the top of
her head and she mumbles something
unintelligible as she gives in to her tiredness.
Minutes later, I follow her into a dreamless sleep.

KAYLEE

In my dream, warm hands are stroking me, smoothing up and down my body and starting fires in their wake. I shiver with desire, a now familiar heat blossoming between my legs, my body recognising the touch even with the haze of sleep still clinging to me.

I open my eyes, letting them adjust to the daylight poking in around the edges of the blinds and they collide with a pair of warm, brown ones.

"Morning, sleeping beauty," Dawson says, kissing me softly. "I'm sorry, did I wake you?" he asks, innocently, his mouth moving to gently bite my earlobe.

"You did," I smile, sleepily. "And what a wonderful way to wake up," I murmur, smoothing my hands down the defined muscles of his back and opening my legs to the delicious invasion of his hips.

His head dips to my breast, pulling a nipple into his mouth and making me gasp as heat shoots straight to my core.

I'm suddenly ripped from the sensual cocoon of Dawson's touch by a loud banging at the door and all at once I'm wide awake.

"Dawson! Kaylee?" Tony's voice joins the banging.

"I'm going to fucking kill him! Who needs birth control when you've got Tony Fucking Cooper!" Dawson curses, leaping out of bed and quickly pulling on his sweatpants and t-shirt before heading downstairs.

I'm hot on his heels, grabbing my discarded robe from the foot of the bed and hitting the top of the stairs just as Dawson throws the door open.

"What the fuck, Tony?" he snarls angrily.

"I've been knocking on your door for five minutes solid!" Tony defends. "It's eleven in the morning, for God's sake! What are you still doing in bed? Never mind, don't answer that." Tony holds his hands up. "I have someone here who wants to see Kaylee."

I'm halfway down the stairs when a curvy woman with midnight black hair suddenly appears from behind Tony and my mouth drops open.

"Meri?"

"Kaylee!" Meri's eyes hone in on me and she pushes past both men, making a bee-line for me as I reach the bottom of the stairs. She throws her arms around me, hugging me tight for an instant, before pushing me away again, hands on her hips as she pins me with a pair of hazel eyes that are currently spitting fire in my direction.

"What the *fuck*, Kaylee?" she says loudly, and I know I'm in deep shit at she calls me by my given name, rather than the nickname she always uses. "Do you have any idea how worried I've been? Remember these?" she asks, sarcastically, holding up her cell phone. "They're called *phones* and when you press these buttons" she stabs at her phone exaggeratedly, "magic happens and you get to call your best friend to let her know you're still alive, not to mention that it also stores all twenty-seven text messages and sixteen voicemails left by said best friend over the last two days, who, by the way, drove here *very* early this morning trying to find you and, holy-sweet-nipples-of-Christ, Kaylee, you better have a fucking good excuse!" Meri finishes, finally running out of breath.

"Meri, I'm so sorry! I've been…busy," I say, lamely.

"Busy?" Meri shouts. "I had visions of you lying dead in a ditch somewhere, or kidnapped by some mafia boss, or forced to become a novelty act in a human circus, or…"

"I'm okay, Meri," I say, cutting her off as I pull the shorter woman into my arms and hug her warmly. "I'm so sorry I worried you and I promise I do have a really good excuse, which I'll tell you all about, just as soon as you calm down."

After a few seconds, Meri's body relaxes, the anger leaving her body as she returns my hug. "Don't ever do that to me again, chick," she whispers, her eyes shining with tears and I know I'm forgiven with the return of my nickname, one she gave me when we were five-years old and I rescued a baby chick and nursed it back to health.

I look over Meri's shoulder to see the two men still standing in the doorway, looking bewildered at the dark-haired force of nature that's just exploded through the door.

"Meri, you remember Dawson? He was a few years above us at high school."

"You're the dude Kaylee tutored for a while," Meri recalls, her eyes sweeping him up and down. "Holy-crap-on-a-cracker, you've changed! Have you grown even taller?" she asks, cranking her head back to look at him.

Dawson smiles at her as he comes to stand next to me, dropping a possessive arm over my shoulder and pulling me against him.

Meri's eyes narrow suspiciously at the easy display of affection as she looks between Dawson and me. "Wait a minute! Have I slipped into a time-warp here? I'm pretty sure it's only been two days and yet, you two look like you've been playing hide the sausage together!"

Guilty color washes over my skin, and even Dawson shifts uncomfortably under Meri's directness.

"Oh, my God! You have!" Meri looks at Dawson. "You must be something special, Dawson, because my girl here was about ready to join a convent."

Dawson pulls me closer and I slip my arms around his waist. "She's the special one, Meri," he says, making my heart flutter, along with a few other places.

Meri's whole demeanour softens as she sees how close we are. "Yeah, she is. I'm glad someone else finally realized it too."

I move away from Dawson, linking my arm with Meri and drawing her into the living area. "How did you find me?" I ask, as Meri sinks down on the sofa with a sigh.

She waves a hand in Tony's direction. "Starsky, here. Or was Hutch the blond one? I never can remember."

I look at Tony, expecting to see his usual grin at Meri's joke, but I'm surprised to see him glowering at her. Interesting. Meri has no filter which doesn't sit well with everyone and I'm beginning to wonder what might have happened on the journey over here with Tony.

"I'll go put some coffee on." Dawson gives me a wink as he heads for the kitchen.

"I'll help you," Tony says, a little too quickly.

As soon as we're alone, Meri wastes no time starting in on me again. "I haven't heard diddly-shit from you since Saturday morning!" she glares at me. "When you didn't answer your texts or messages I got scared. After the way you've been behaving lately, you left me no choice but to track you down and this was the only place I could think that you'd come."

"I'm so sorry, Meri," I apologise again, sitting down next to her. "I thought I put my phone in my rucksack, but I was in a hurry and must have left it on my bed at home. Coming here was a bit of a knee jerk reaction after what happened at Jake's."

"Jake's?" Meri asks, confused.

I tell Meri about my disastrous visit to Jake's apartment and my confrontation with Prue.

Meri sighs. "Okay, not your best idea ever," she says, with her usual honesty, "but I'm sure you know that already without me rubbing it in. Is that why you took off?"

I sigh. "It was everything, Meri. When I got home, the house was so cold and empty. I felt like I was teetering on the edge of an emotional black hole and the phone call I had from Veronica just pushed me over."

Meri looks as if she's got a bad smell under her nose. "Wait, what now? Veronica? What did Little Miss Control Freak want this time?"

"She rang to tell me I was fired from the squad."

"She did what?" Meri shrieks. "That bitch never liked you! What were the reasons for firing you?"

"For unacceptable behavior that reflected badly on the whole squad," I say, repeating Veronica's words.

"Well, that's a double fucking standard if ever I heard one!" Meri says, echoing my own thoughts. "You're far from the only one on the squad who's broken the rules when it comes to drinking and partying. Everyone knows how often Veronica's used her position as choreographer with the Cubs to get into parties no one would let her skanky ass into otherwise, not to mention those two players she's been fucking!"

"I know, and I told her as much, said she needed to take a good, hard look at herself before she started throwing accusations my way. Then she called me a fucking bitch and told me I was done on the cheer squad, that confirmation of my termination was already in the mail."

Meri looks like she's ready to pop. "So, it was already a done deal and she just wanted the pleasure of telling you? I swear to God next time I see that woman I'm going to ram her porcelain teeth so far down her throat she'll be shitting them for a week!"

I can't help but smile at the visual. "You know what, though? Afterward, the only thing I could think about was the face of a little girl in the crowd at the last home game. Her eyes were full of adoration, the look of a young girl who thought I had the best job in the whole world. What a fucking joke! What kind of shitty role model have

I been to that young girl and all the other young girls with stars in their eyes?"

"Listen, chick, this is fate," Meri states matter-of-factly. "This is your chance to change direction. I mean, I know you loved cheerleading at high school, but it was never meant to become a professional career. Vet school was the dream, remember?"

"I remember," I sigh, knowing Meri's right.

"Look on the bright side. At least your farts won't clear a room now you don't have to eat all that high protein shit!" Meri snorts, and we both burst out laughing.

"Seriously though, now it's time for you figure out what you want, so you can move on with your life. Don't be afraid to start over, it's a chance to rebuild your life the way you wanted all along. Life isn't always about finding yourself, sometimes it's about creating yourself."

I feel the sting of tears at the back of my eyes as I hug Meri tightly. "Thank you," I whisper. A thought suddenly occurs to me as I release her. "How did you find me? I mean, how did you know I was here with Dawson?"

Meri shrugs. "I didn't. When I got here, I went straight to the police station and bumped into blond and brooding, there." She nods toward the kitchen. "I told him who I was, and he said he'd bring me here. We had a very nice conversation in the car on the ride over," she grins wickedly.

"Oh, God, what did you say to him?" I ask, dreading the answer.

"I only said he was hot, for an older guy," Meri says, innocently. "And I may have asked him if he had a licence to carry a weapon that large."

"Oh, Meri! Why do you do that? You do realize that one of these days, someone's going to see through your smart mouth, don't you?"

"Nah! People don't look that deep," Meri replies, confidently.

Meri doesn't do anything by halves, but she has the biggest heart and is fiercely loyal. I'm one of the very few people who knows the sadness that lies beneath the blunt humor and easy quips she uses like a shield.

"So, spill, chick! What the fudge is going on with Lev? Tony wouldn't tell me anything on the way over."

I give Meri a quick run-down of everything that's happened over the last few days, telling her about the attack on Prue and my upcoming visit to see Lev. Her face pales when I get to the part about the child-trafficking business we're trying to get information on.

"That's just...hideous!" Meri says, with tears in her eyes. "Are you really sure you want to go through with it?"

"More than ever. At first, I wanted to go and see Lev for myself, but it's so much more than what I want now. I have to do it if there's any chance of stopping those monsters hurting any more innocent children."

Meri reaches for my hand. "I know, chick, and I'm so proud of you. Look at you, all grown up," she teases. "So, when are you going to see him?"

"In the next day or so, I think. Tony is organizing everything in Daryl's absence and Dawson's been kind enough to let me stay here."

"Oh, I don't think kindness has anything to do with it!" Meri smirks. "So, have you two...uh..." Meri makes a circle with her thumb and index finger, poking the finger of her other hand through the middle.

I roll my eyes. "Seriously, Meri! How old are you?"

"Older than you, and the rules are you have to tell me every dirty, little detail," Meri says, tongue-in-cheek.

"Only by ten months, and no chance!" I retort, returning her grin.

"You two look right together," Meri says. "I'm really happy for you, chick."

"Thanks, honey. It's all happened so fast, but Dawson is amazing. I still can't believe it was him that answered the call."

Meri holds her hands to her heart and flutters her lashes. "Ah, the wonder of fate."
I laugh. "Yeah, yeah! Listen, I'm just gonna quickly put some clothes on." I ignore Meri's knowing smile as I head upstairs.

I throw on some sweatpants and a t-shirt, quickly brushing my teeth and putting my hair up in a ponytail. I come back downstairs just Dawson and Tony are walking into the room with mugs of coffee and a plate of cookies, which they place on the table before each taking a chair.

"I'm assuming you've filled Meri in on everything?" Tony asks, as I sit down next to her on the sofa again.

I nod. "Yes. Meri would never say or do anything to put me in danger."

Tony's eyes flick to Meri with an odd intensity. "I can see that. It's a pretty special thing to have friends who've got your back like that."

"We've known each other since kindergarten," Meri says. "Been through everything together." She leans forward to grab her mug of coffee at the same time as Tony, and their hands touch accidentally. "Sorry," Meri mumbles, withdrawing her hand as if she's been burned, a rare blush creeping into her cheeks.

Tony looks just as uncomfortable, clearing his throat before speaking again.

"Everything's arranged for tomorrow afternoon" he says, looking at me.

"Tomorrow?" I feel nervous now that I know it's really going to happen.

"I'll be there too," Dawson says. "Neither of us will be able to go into the visiting room with you, but we'll be just outside the whole time."

The thought of having Dawson with me goes a long way to alleviating some of my nervousness.

"So, how did Lev take the news that he has a daughter?"

"Pretty much as we expected," Tony replies. "Called me a…well, let's just say he didn't believe me until he saw the proof," he says, dryly.

"So, the DNA test…?"

"Proved you are most definitely his daughter," Tony confirms.

"Oh, wow! I guess I always had that little bit of doubt, you know?"

"Well, there's no doubt about it now," Tony says.

"So, does he want to meet me?" I ask.

"He does. Although he's not making any us any promises with regards to information. For now, he's just agreed to the meeting, so it may involve you seeing him more than once. Are you up for that?"

"Can I decide once I've seen him tomorrow?" I ask, looking over at Dawson, his expression making it very clear that he's not happy with that idea in the slightest.

"This is your call, Kaylee. You can see him tomorrow and then walk away if you choose to. I gave you my word that you wouldn't have to do anything you didn't want to, and I intend to stand by that."

Meri raises her chin in Tony's direction. "So, you're telling us that if Kaylee doesn't get anything of value to you from daddykins tomorrow, you're just going to let her walk away from it all?"

"If that's what she decides, yes," Tony replies, looking directly at her and after several seconds Meri is the first to drop her gaze. Unheard of.

"Can you stay?" I ask Meri, hopefully.

"Only tonight. There's no way I'm making the drive back today, so I'm booked in at a local hotel. I really need to get back for a meeting with a client tomorrow afternoon but if you need me to stay…?"

"No, no, it's fine," I say, hiding my disappointment. Meri works for an interior designer who she has a great working relationship with and I know she would've hated leaving Sasha in the lurch to come here today, which makes me feel guilty all over again.

"Okay, if you're sure," Meri says. "Besides, I'm pretty sure you've got all the protection you need with these two," she smiles, looking between Tony and Dawson.

"Are you sure you'll be okay staying at a hotel? I mean, maybe you could stay here, if Dawson doesn't mind?" I say, my gaze swinging to him in question.

"No, it's fine really," Meri says, quickly. "Besides, something tells me you two lovebirds need your privacy," she adds, with a saucy wink in Dawson's direction.

I'm mesmerised as Dawson throws back his head and laughs, my eyes clinging lovingly to his face.

"I like you, Meri," he grins. "Your honesty is like a breath of fresh air!"

"I like you too, Dawson," Meri smiles in return. "All ten feet of you. How tall are you anyway? Doesn't your head get cold up there?"

"Six-five, and that's why I grew the beard. The extra warmth comes in handy," Dawson chuckles, and I can't help thinking it comes in handy for other things too.

"Well, much as I *love* talking about Dawson's beard, I need to get back to work," Tony says, draining the remaining coffee from his mug and standing up. "Are you coming with, Meri, or...?"

"Stay for lunch," Dawson says, "You and Kaylee can spend some time together I'm sure Tony won't mind coming back for you later, will you Tony?"

"Why would I mind?" Tony asks, sarcastically. "I've only got a mountain of my own paperwork, not to mention Daryl's, along with a load of loose ends to tie up ready for tom...."

"Great! That's sorted then," Dawson interrupts, standing up to slap Tony on the back.

"Just remember who got you where you are today, detective," Tony says, glowering. "I'll be back to pick you up around six, Meri. Make sure you're ready."

"I will, Sire," Meri says, standing to give him a little curtsy.

With one final, disgusted look, Tony turns on his heel and heads for the front door, slamming it behind him.

We order in pizza for lunch and eat it straight from the box, not even bothering to sit at the table, Dawson and I sprawled on the sofa and Meri in one of the chairs.

We spend the afternoon talking, laughing and enjoying a few beers while we play cards. It's one of the best afternoons of my life, in the company of two of my favorite people in the whole world.

Meri and Dawson get along like a house on fire and I have a suspicion he's one of the few people who sees through her bluster to the person hiding underneath.

When Tony returns at exactly six, he seems in a better mood than he did when he left. I hug Meri tightly as she leaves, making sure she has both Dawson and Tony's cell numbers, so she can keep in touch.

Meri gives me a final squeeze at the door. "Love you, chick. I'll be thinking of you and waiting by the phone tomorrow."

"Love you too, honey. Thank you for coming to rescue me." I smile, returning her hug.

"Always," Meri says, releasing me. "Whenever, wherever, just like Shakira said."

"I'll pick you up tomorrow afternoon at three," Tony says, before turning to follow Meri as she heads toward the car.

Dawson comes to stand behind me, wrapping his arms around my waist and I lean back against him as we watch Tony and Meri drive off, already missing her.

"Remind me never to cross her where you're concerned," Dawson murmurs, his lips finding a sensitive spot behind my ear and making me shiver.

I turn to face him, linking my arms around his neck. "She's a soft touch once you get to know her."

"Something tells me there's more to Meri than meets the eye," Dawson says, his instincts sharp.

"Yeah. Remind me to tell you about it sometime. Right now, I need food."

"You're hungry again?" Dawson asks in surprise.

"Hey, don't knock it, buster. You need to indulge me. I've got two years-worth of food groups to catch up on."

"Oh, I'm more than happy to indulge you," Dawson smirks, dipping his head to mine and kissing me soundly. His hands slide around to cup my ass, pulling me against him so I can feel his erection pressing between my thighs.

"Steady on there, detective," I murmur. "Anyone would think you're happy to see me."

"Baby, I'm always happy to see you," Dawson chuckles, dropping a quick kiss on my lips. Come on, sunshine. Let's get you fed."

We make tuna sandwiches with salad and a bowl of chips, crashing on the sofa to eat while we half-watch an action movie on cable.

"Did you notice Tony was a bit...off today?" I ask, my head resting on Dawson's chest.

"No more of a dick than normal," Dawson says. "Although, thinking about it, I guess he did seem a little short-tempered."

"I thought he was acting a little odd around Meri. You don't think...?"

"Tony and Meri?" Dawson says in disbelief.

"He's like, twenty years older than she is!"

"Sixteen," I correct. "I just thought I saw something between them. I was probably imagining it," I shrug.

"Tony will never settle down again," Dawson says, confidently. "Especially not with someone so much younger than him."

"Again?"

"Yeah, he was married for several years."

"Tony was married?" I shift my weight so I'm looking at Dawson. "Wow! I just assumed he was a confirmed bachelor."

"He is now, despite his charm with the women."

"So, what happened? Did they divorce?" I ask, curiously.

"She died."

"Oh, no!" My hand flies to my mouth in shock.

"He never talks about it," Dawson says. "It happened before we met. All I know is that she was also a cop and was shot in the line of duty."

"That's...tragic," I say, my heart aching for Tony. "Just goes to show, you never really know what someone else has been through."

"Tony's one of the best people I know," Dawson says. "Sure, we give each other shit, but we've always had each other's backs. The respect I have for him is the only reason I didn't knock his lights out when he told us about the plan for you and Lev."

"You could've fooled me! You were channelling some serious anger in the ring yesterday," I say.

"Nothing he didn't deserve," Dawson smirks. "Talking of Lev, you feeling okay about tomorrow?"

"Nervous about finally meeting him, seeing him in the flesh. If Lev is the monster that everyone says he is, what does that make me? Which of his traits have I inherited?"

Dawson strokes my hair back from my face. "Lev is a product of his experiences when he was under cover. He's driven and ambitious, but he made a choice to use those traits in negative ways. You choose to use those strengths positively and selflessly. Our characteristics don't define us but the way we choose to use them does."

"You're good at this listening stuff," I grin, pulling his head down to mine for a lingering kiss before snuggling back into his chest. "I'm glad you'll be with me tomorrow," I murmur, sleepily. "It makes the whole thing less scary."

"Me too, baby," Dawson murmurs.

The warmth of his body and the soothing touch of his fingers in my hair makes my eyelids heavy and I close my eyes with a contented sigh.

I'm woken sometime later by the sensation of weightlessness as Dawson carries me to bed.

"I'm sorry. I feel asleep," I say drowsily, protesting the loss of his warmth as he places me on the bed.

"You went out like a light," Dawson murmurs, helping me out of my clothes before undressing himself and climbing in next to me, pulling the covers over us. I automatically burrow into him, seeking the familiar warmth and comfort of his body.

"I love you, Dawson," I sigh, before giving in to sleep once more.

☐

Kaylee

A sombre-faced Tony briefs me on the journey over, telling me Lev and I will be alone in the visiting area apart from the two guards, one on my side and one on Lev's. Both he and Dawson will be able to see and hear everything via a special screen linked to the security cameras on the walls.

Tony's acting strangely, not quite making eye contact when he speaks to me, particularly when I ask him if Meri got to her hotel okay the night before, and I make a mental note to ask her about it when I call her later.

The journey to the prison is uneventful, with Dawson riding alongside Tony while I take the backseat. As we drive through the prison gates, I remember how, just three days ago, I was sitting on the ground outside, feeling lost and alone, wondering which way to turn next. I'm surprised to see one of the same guards on duty and wonder if he recognises me as the unstable blond who stamped her feet and demanded to be let in.

Papers are signed, and I'm searched thoroughly in processing before Dawson gives me a bone-crushing hug and I'm following one of the guards through to the visiting area.

I walk to the last booth, taking a seat on the metal stool that's bolted to the floor. There are partitions on either side of me which give the illusion of privacy, but I know if there were other people in here, I'd be able to hear every word they said to their loved ones. I look around, seeing the two cameras Tony referred to and give one of them a nervous smile, knowing both men can see me.

I smooth my sweaty palms down the front of my black skinny jeans, fiddling with the buttons on the long sleeved pink blouse, knowing I'm fidgeting but unable to stop. I look at the glass window in front of me, staring at the little sign in the corner that reads:

'Keep your hands visible at all times'

Abruptly, I place my hands on the counter in front of me, noticing their tremor, taking deep breaths to calm my racing heart. I know Dawson and Tony are less than ten feet away on the other side of the door, but right now it feels more like ten miles as I sit waiting for a man who has committed some unforgivable crimes. Waiting for my father.

My head snaps up at the sound of a door opening, my heart climbing into my throat as I wait for my first glimpse of Lev. Instinctively, I stand up, not wanting to be at a height disadvantage when I first meet him.

The photographs I've seen online don't do him justice. He's much taller in person than any of those photographs could convey, and there's an innate confidence in the way he walks, how he holds himself, as he approaches the glass. He's dressed in a grey and white striped prison suit, his clenched hands cuffed in front of him, neither of which does anything to diminish the intimidating aura that clings to him like a second skin.

His blue eyes bore into mine through the glass as the guard accompanying him removes his handcuffs. The intensity of that look scares me, making me feel like he can see into my very soul.

The guard moves to the back of the room to stand against the wall, his expression blank, and Lev sweeps a hand in front of him, indicating that I should sit first. I lower myself back to my seat on shaky legs as he reaches for the white telephone screwed to the wall, and I follow suit, holding the counterpart to my ear.

"Guess I didn't need that DNA test, after all," Lev says, his voice deep and gravelly.
"You look exactly like her, same shaped face, same nose, same long blonde hair. But you have my eyes and my chin."

He's right about the eyes as we both have the exact same eye shape, the same shade of blue. "I assume by 'her', you mean my birth mother?"

"Maria. Her name was Maria," Lev states, and there's something in his voice when he says her name, a tiny flicker of warmth in his eyes for just a second. "She was beautiful."

It's good to have even the few meagre details Lev has just given me as I start to build an image of my mother in my head. "Why didn't she tell you she was pregnant? Why did she run from you?"

"Is that what they told you? That she ran from me?" Lev asks, a bitter twist to his mouth. "Yes, I suppose that's what they would say," he murmurs, answering his own question. "What is it you want to hear, Kaylee? That we were madly in love, that I would have given my life for her, and she for me? Is that the perfect little story you want?"

"I just want the truth, Lev," I say, using his name for the first time.

"Lev?" he says, in mock horror. "Come on now, princess. Not *daddy* or *dad*? I'll even settle for *father*."

I try to keep my temper in check. "That title has to be earned, not demanded."

"Kids today, no fucking respect." Lev sighs, pursing his lips, his eyes narrowing as he looks at me. "You want the truth? Believe me, little girl, you can't handle the truth."

"Try me!" I snap, losing the rein on my temper. "Unless you only agreed to see me, so you can play your silly little mind games, boost your enormous ego by proving you're the one in control!"

"I don't need to prove anything to anyone. Look where I am," Lev says, spreading his hands wide. "I'm not going anywhere. Not for a long time, if the prosecution has anything to do with it. I've been a bad, bad boy, or didn't they tell you that either?"

"If you're going to behave like an asshole, what are we doing here wasting our time?" I ask, frustrated.

"You tell me," Lev counters. "What exactly are you hoping for? An emotional reunion? Some father daughter bonding in prison? Or, maybe you want to hear how much I regret not being a part of your life, how much I'd like to make up for all the precious years we missed out on," he says, mockingly.

"No, I just expected a man with your intelligence to act like an adult, not a spoiled five-year-old with a gigantic chip on his shoulder," I say, bluntly. "You sit there like the world owes you a fucking favor, when in actual fact, the opposite is true. When I agreed to come here, I promised myself I'd keep an open mind, withhold judgement until I met you myself. And now that I have, I realize you're not the man they told me you were. You're actually worse." I get to my feet, knowing this is a lost cause. "Thanks for the closure," I say, starting to replace the phone.

"Sit down, Kaylee."

I hesitate at the command. "Why? What more could we possibly have to say to each other? I'll just chalk today down to yet another life-enriching experience, despite the huge disappointment you turned out to be."

"You just gonna keep running your mouth, princess, or are you going to sit your ass back down and listen?" Lev says, a note of steel in his voice. "Play your cards right, and I may even give you what you came here for," he adds, dangling the golden carrot, and it's probably the only thing he could have said that would make me do as he's asked.

I sit down, glaring at him through the glass.

"Good, girl. That wasn't so hard, now was it?" he says, with a self-satisfied smile.
I swallow the anger that's burning up my throat, the desire for information warring against the need to leave.

I ignore his patronising tone. "How did you meet my mother?"

Lev considers me for a minute before answering. "She was the wife of the man I was working to bring down. I spent two years infiltrating his organisation, earning his trust by doing things you can't even imagine."

"What kind of things?" I ask, pretty sure I'm not going to like the answer but wanting to know everything, no matter how bad.

"If Gabriel needed information, I got it. If he needed someone dead, I made it happen. He wanted someone who would do his bidding, no questions asked, to the point that when he told me to prove my loyalty by cutting off my own finger, I asked which one," he says, holding up his right hand where his pinkie finger is missing.

"May not seem like much to some, losing a finger, but it was Gabriel's way of making sure I was his man."

I close my eyes, swallowing the bile that rises in my throat at the thought of Lev severing his own finger. "I don't understand. You were a cop! You were supposed to be upholding the law, not breaking it!"

"Ah, how wonderful it must be, living in your world," Lev says, closing his eyes in mock bliss. "To feel so righteous, seeing the world in shades of black and white, good and bad." His eyes open abruptly, and he looks directly at me. "I hate to break it to you, princess, but the world is full of gray. Good people do bad shit when it suits them, and vice versa. Kind of muddies the water, doesn't it? I did what I needed to do to get the job done."

"You keep telling yourself that and one day you might believe it. Seems to me you enjoyed it all a little too much," I say, and he frowns. "So, how does Maria fit into all this?"

"Gabriel introduced her to me one night at a party at his house. I thought she was the most beautiful woman I'd ever seen." Lev says, a faraway look in his eyes. "I wanted her from the moment I laid eyes on her, and it was mutual. We fought our feelings for a while, knowing how dangerous it would be for us to start anything, but it was inevitable that we would give in eventually."

"Did you love her?" I ask, and for a minute I don't think he's going to answer.

"Yes. Very much. Enough to break all the rules and risk my cover, tell her the real reason I was there. She knew what kind of business Gabriel was running and she was terrified of him, lived in fear of his erratic moods and his...particular form of punishment where she was concerned. I don't think she had any idea of the world that awaited her when she married him. Yet, despite what she'd been through, there was still an innocence about her, a hopefulness," Lev says, lost in memories. "Then, one night, after we'd been seeing each other for several months, she came to me, desperate, saying she couldn't take it anymore, living in fear every day and having to hide our relationship. She wanted us to run away from it all, begged me to leave with her, go somewhere he'd never find us."

"Why didn't you?" I ask, breathlessly, hanging on Lev's every word.

"Because I knew as long as Gabriel was drawing breath, he would wouldn't stop until he found us. No one crossed Gabriel. Not ever. Maybe if I'd remembered that, things would've turned out differently."

"What do you mean?" I ask, desperately wanting him to continue the story.

Lev smiles and sits back on his stool. "Sadly, our time is up for today. If you want to know more, you'll come back tomorrow.".

"But…wait! Don't you want to know anything about me?" I ask desperately, trying to keep him talking.

Lev glances up at the camera behind me with a small smile. "I already know everything I need to about you, Kaylee. I was sorry to hear that you recently lost your adoptive parents. That must be hard for you," he says, looking genuinely sympathetic. "They took their faith very seriously and you're really quite sheltered due to your strict upbringing. Your father ran the family accountancy business, and you helped out part time, when you weren't cheering for the California Cubs."

I can feel the color draining from my face, my mouth hanging open as Lev lays my life out in front of me.

"Your best friend is called Meredith Greene, although you call her Meri for short," Lev continues. "You made an application to a vet school here in Modesto, but later withdrew it and settled for becoming a glorified…dancer instead, although they fired you a few days ago for inappropriate behavior. You achieved exceptional grades at school, so I can't imagine why you would choose cheerleading over veterinary school, unless your parents were trying to prevent you from coming here in case you bumped into your old dad."

"How did you…?"

"How did I know all that?" Lev anticipates my question. "I may be in here, princess, but I still have contacts, people who bring me information about the outside world."

Lev turns and nods his head at the guard behind him, who moves forward to secure the handcuffs around his wrists again. "I'll expect you at the same time tomorrow." Without a backward glance, Lev turns and walks out of the room.

"I can't believe you agreed to see him again tomorrow!" Dawson scowls, once we're all in the car and headed home. "He already knows far more about you than I'm comfortable with!"
I sigh, rubbing my hand tiredly across my eyes and sinking into the luxurious leather backseat of

Tony's car. "We knew this was a possibility, Dawson. I can't stop now. Lev was really starting to open up there at the end. I don't care if it means one more visit, or another ten, I've started this and I intend to finish it."

Dawson glares at me, and I realize it's the first time I've been on the receiving end of his anger. I can feel the tears pricking the back of my eyes and I swallow hard, determined not to break down.

The rest of the journey passes in strained silence, Dawson's bad mood filling the car like a dark cloud. Tony drops us outside the house and after a quick goodbye, I'm inside and up the stairs the second Dawson opens the door, ignoring him as he calls my name and heading for the spare room. I close the door firmly behind me and sink down on the bed, my nerves and emotions in shreds.

If I thought a closed door was going to keep Dawson out, I'm sadly mistaken, and he comes barrelling into the room, looking pissed, his large frame making the space feel small. "You do realize that he's playing you, don't you?" he asks, angrily.

"Have you considered that maybe I'm playing him too?" I retort. "That I've learned more about my past in the last few hours than I have in the last month?"

"And you believed him?" Dawson asks, incredulously.

"Yes, Dawson, I believed him! What does he stand to gain by lying to me? He's in prison, awaiting a trial which will most likely see him go down for life. What reason would he have for fabricating some story about the past?"

"Why do you think, Kaylee? To pass the time, fuck with your head! You heard Tony the other day, he's an expert when it comes to manipulation and getting what he wants. He finds a way to turn every situation to his own advantage, only this time you're the one who's going to end up getting hurt!" Dawson growls.

"Even if that's true, it's my decision to make and I'm prepared to take that risk if there's a even the tiniest chance that I can get Lev to talk! You may have forgotten, but this isn't just about me anymore!" I yell.

"It *is* about you, Kaylee! That's *all* it's about as far as I'm concerned! What the fuck am I supposed to do? Just stand back, keep my mouth shut? Let the woman I love put herself at risk?" Dawson shouts.

My mouth falls open as I look him. "What did you just say?"

"Which part?" he asks, still angry.

I can hardly breathe. "The woman I love part."

All the anger suddenly drains from him, as he realizes what he's just said. "That's not the way I wanted to tell you," he sighs, raking his hands through his hair in frustration. "Last night, as you fell asleep, you told me you loved me and hearing you say it floored me, because I know I feel the same way. I love you, Kaylee, and the thought of you being hurt, of anything happening to you…" He swallows, trying to regain his composure.

I stand and walk to him, cupping his face in my hands and bringing his mouth to mine so I can kiss him. "I love you too, Dawson, more than I ever thought was possible in just a matter of days," I say, pulling back to look at him. "But this thing with Lev is something I have to do, and I can't do it alone. I need you with me on this, need the strength you give me. The whole time I was in that room with Lev today, I knew you were waiting for me outside and that thought kept me going, because there's nowhere safer for me than here with you, in your arms."

Dawson crushes me to him and I hold him to me just as fiercely, needing him closer, wanting to climb inside him and stay like that forever.

Dawson presses his forehead to mine. "I'm sorry, baby. I just see red where you're concerned. The thought of anyone hurting you makes me want to break things," he says, gruffly. "But, whatever you need, I'm there for you. We'll get through this together, and the rest we'll work out as we go along."

I kiss him again. "Thank you," I whisper against his mouth, taking his hand and tugging him toward his bedroom, *our* bedroom.

I stop next to the bed, pulling my blouse over my head and unclipping my bra. My jeans are next as I slide them down my legs, followed by my panties, until I'm completely naked in front of him. I move to lie in the middle of the bed, stretching my arms above my head, my body completely open to him.

"I want to make love with you, Dawson," I whisper.

Dawson sucks in a breath at my words, his chest rising and falling heavily as his eyes roam my body hungrily. His hands go to his t-shirt, ripping it over his head before unbuttoning and kicking off his jeans and boxers. My eyes drink him in, trailing from his broad shoulders and ripped abs down to his thick shaft, already swollen with desire.

He joins me on the bed, lowering his body to mine and I open my legs to accommodate him as our mouths collide in a frenzy of need. I can't get enough of him, and it seems the feeling is mutual as Dawson crushes me to him, his weight pressing me into the mattress.

"Turn over," I whisper, and Dawson rolls onto his back, bringing me with him so I'm straddling his hips. I trail my hands across his chest, tracing his tattoos as my thumbs skim over his nipples. Dawson groans, the muscles in his jaw clenching as I repeat the caress, bending forward to flick my tongue over the tight nubs before working my way down his body. My lips tease over the ridges of his abs, nibbling and biting as I go, until my mouth is hovering over his throbbing shaft.

Instinctively, my tongue flicks out, licking the moisture from the tip, tasting the saltiness of his fluid, before repeating the motion again and then again, encouraged by Dawson's groans.

I raise uncertain eyes to his, quickly reassured by the desire on his face. "Show me what to do," I say, before taking him in my mouth.

"Oh, God! You're doing just fine on your own, baby!" Dawson chokes, his hips jerking uncontrollably at my touch, and I'm shocked at how his pleasure feeds my own as moisture pools between my legs.

Dawson hands cup my head, showing me how to move up and down on him, finding a rhythm as I take as much of his length in my mouth as I can. My tongue swirls around the end of his shaft and he nearly comes up off the bed, his hips making little thrusts as he pushes himself deeper into the warmth of my mouth.

"You need to stop, baby. I don't want to cum in your mouth, not this time," he pants, and I release his swollen length reluctantly as he pulls me back up toward him, sliding his body down as he does, so that I'm straddling his face. Before I can ask what he's doing, his mouth fastens on me, opening me up to the swipe of his tongue on my clit. Any embarrassment I feel at such an intimate position slips away as his mouth works its magic on my sensitive flesh, making me cry out as I move against the delicious friction of his tongue. It doesn't take long before I can feel the electric shocks working their way up my spine as my orgasm builds, and with a superhuman effort I lift myself away from his mouth, sliding back down his body to straddle his hips again.

"I want to cum with you inside me, like before," I say, breathlessly, reaching between us to grasp him in my hand, sliding the tip of him along my wet folds as I coat him with my juices. I sink down on him slowly, giving my body time to adjust to his length and girth as my hips rise and fall against him until he's fully submerged within me.

The sensation of him filling me up is exquisite and we're both gasping as I begin to ride him, Dawson's fingers digging almost painfully into my hips as he thrusts up into my welcoming body, making me cry out with pleasure.

"That's it, baby!" Dawson gasps, as our bodies come together in a frantic rhythm, the sounds of our lovemaking loud in the quiet of the room.

I shift my weight, finding the right position so that his body hits mine in just the right spot with each thrust of his hips and within seconds I fly over the edge, barely aware that I'm sobbing out my pleasure as with one final surge, Dawson chokes out his orgasm and I feel his hot seed filling me up.

I collapse against his chest, trying to catch my breath as I come down from the high of my physical release. Dawson rolls us onto our sides so we're facing each other, pressing soft kisses to my cheeks, my eyes, my mouth. I feel his chest rumble with laughter and I draw back to look at him.

"What's so funny?"

"Just remembering how you told Lev Sarado, drugs baron, to grow the fuck up," he chuckles.

"Yep. I totally schooled his ass," I grin.

"That's my girl," Dawson smiles, dropping a kiss on the end of my nose.

I suddenly remember something. "Can I use your phone? I need to call Meri."

"Sure. You want some privacy?"

"No, stay."

Dawson rolls away from me, plucking his phone from the pocket of his jeans on the floor. He unlocks it and dials Meri's number, handing it to me and propping himself up on his elbow to face me.

Meri answers on the second ring, immediately bombarding me with questions. "Hey chick, what gives? Are you okay? How did it go? What's he like?"

"Whoa, slow down!" I chuckle, and proceed to fill Meri in on my time with Lev.

"He sounds...intimidating," Meri says. "You sure you're okay?"

"Yeah, I'm good. Dawson's here with me." I reach out to stroke his face with my free hand, my fingers tracing his beard, closing my eyes as Dawson nibbles at my palm.

"Was the hotel okay?"

"Yeah, sure, why wouldn't it be?" Meri says, defensively.

"Is everything okay, Meri? I asked Tony this morning if you got back to your hotel okay and he could barely look at me. Did something happen between you two?" I ask, seeing Dawson frown at my question.

"Don't be ridiculous! He's much too old for me!" she scoffs.

"I meant, did you have an argument?"

"Oh! No. No arguments," Meri says, evasively. "Listen, I have to go. I'm going with Mom and dad to visit Rory."

I sigh, feeling the sorrow that always steals over me at the mention of Meri's brother. "Okay, honey. I love you."

"Love you too, chick."

I end the call, staring thoughtfully at the phone. Meri's acting weird, and when this is all over with Lev, I have every intention of finding out why.

"Everything okay?" Dawson asks, seeing my frown.

"I'm not sure. Meri's hiding something from me," I reply.

"I'm sure it's nothing to worry about. Meri's a big girl. She'll tell you when she's ready. She probably doesn't want to offload on you right now," he says, smoothing his hand over my bare hip.

"Yeah, you're right," I say, leaning forward to kiss him and parking my worry to one side. For now.

"Come on," he says, digging his fingers into my ribs and I shriek as he tickles me.

"Let's go shower, before you spring a leak again."

"Ouch! Low blow!" I pout, my eyes clinging to him lovingly as he leaps out of bed.

"Nothing like the blow you gave me earlier," he leers, walking around the bed and yanking me to my feet, chuckling at the color that heats my cheeks. "I love making you blush," he says, tugging me toward the bathroom. "Come on, I'll scrub your back if you scrub mine."

As it turns out, we scrub a lot more than each other's backs, which ends up with us both in a tangle of limbs on the bathroom floor, breathing hard and totally spent.

"I didn't know you could do that with a loofah," I gasp.

"Neither did I," Dawson chuckles, nuzzling my neck. "I love you, Kaylee."

"Love you too, Dawson."

DAWSON

"Now, remember, we'll be watching you through the security cameras, like before," Tony says. "Yesterday was about establishing a dialogue between you both. His agenda was meeting you, figuring you out, seeing if you were worth the investment of any more of his time. Luckily for us, it seems you were."

"Go me!" Kaylee says, half-heartedly.

I can see she's on edge by the cute little tick she gets in the corner of her mouth whenever she's nervous. I pull her into my arms, hugging her tightly before bending to kiss her, my mouth lingering on hers. "I'll be waiting for you, sunshine," I promise, stealing another quick kiss before reluctantly letting her go.

I look across at Tony, fully expecting one of his usual sarcastic quips at our display of affection, but he just stands there with his hands in his pockets, his expression thoughtful.

"Right, well, I guess I'll see you both later," Kaylee says, turning to follow the guard through to the visiting area, and for some reason, the sound of the door closing behind her seems final.

The room we're waiting in is small and windowless, the only furniture a table and two chairs, which Tony and I take a seat in. Tony clicks the small, black monitor screen into a stand on the table and plugs in the earphones, passing one set to me, before placing the others in his own ears. He flips through the touch-screen, pressing various buttons, and the live feed from the security cameras appears.

Lev is already waiting on the other side of the glass as Kaylee takes a seat at the booth, looking as if he doesn't have a care in the world despite where he is and what he's done. He reaches to his left and picks up the phone on the wall, bringing it to his ear.

"Good to see you again, princess," he says, and something about the way he says the word princess sets my teeth on edge.

"Lev," Kaylee replies, with a slight nod.

"Still no *daddy*? Disappointing," Lev sighs.

"Are we really going to do this again?" Kaylee says, sounding exasperated. "I thought we moved past all this shit yesterday."

"You're no fun!" Lev smirks. "Straight to business then. Where were we? Ah, yes! Maria wanted us to leave, but I was reluctant, knowing what the repercussions would be if Gabriel found out. So, I convinced her we were better off leaving things the way they were, or at least I thought I had. Unfortunately, Maria had other plans."

"What do you mean?"

"The next morning, she was gone. Just...disappeared. Gabriel was furious, tore the house apart looking for her. She was his wife, but she was also a possession, and Gabriel didn't like to lose his possessions. So, as his most trusted man, I was given the job of finding her. Bringing her back."

"And did you? Find her, I mean?" Kaylee asks.

"Yes, but not for several months. Months of hell, wondering if she was okay, trying not to reveal my true feelings in front of Gabriel. I checked airports, train stations, bus depots, every form of transport known to man, but she covered her tracks well. Every time I thought I was getting close, I hit another dead end. I later found out she had help from one of her father's men."

"Sounds like he did Maria a huge favor." Kaylee says. "Where was she?"

"Still in California. Hiding in plain sight. I cast the net far and wide looking for her, and didn't think for one minute she'd be hiding under our noses," Lev grimaces. "I tracked her to an apartment on the coast in Santa Barbara. I left straight away, giving Gabriel some story about a potential contact there. I didn't want anyone else to know where she was until I had chance to talk to her myself."

"How did she react when she saw you again?" Kaylee asks, curiosity coloring her voice.

"She cried. She was even more beautiful than I remembered and our feelings for each other were still as strong as when she left. We had important things to discuss, details to work out, questions I needed answers to, but that was all forgotten the minute we saw each other again."

Lev pauses and looks at me. "I'm sure you don't want to hear all the gory details, do you princess? Must be uncomfortable hearing about mummy and daddy getting it on," he smirks.

"Don't be a dick, Lev. I do know people have sex! I'm almost twenty-one-years-old, not five!" she snaps.

I can't help my small smile at her words, knowing that my girl isn't quite as knowledgeable about sex as she likes to make out, but enjoying hearing her put him in his place.

"So you are, and very mature at that," Lev agrees, and I'm sure I'm imagining the tiny spark of admiration I see in his eyes.

"What happened after the sex?" Kaylee asks, bluntly.

Lev chuckles at her frankness. "This is the best part of the whole story. The glorious finale," he says, as if he's performing to an audience. "Seems someone tipped off Gabriel and he followed me. He caught us together, pulled a gun on me..."

Kaylee's looks distressed at Lev's words. "Oh God, no!"

"Figured it out haven't you, princess? Maria threw herself at him and the gun went off. The bullet lodged in her chest, here," Lev says, holding his free hand against the left side of his chest. "If it had gone clean through, I would've been dead too. Gabriel would've had a two-for-one," he says, his mouth twisting with bitterness. "She died instantly, everything she was, gone in a second. I watched her blood seep across the floor, looked into her empty eyes that had been so full of life and love only minutes before, but she was gone," Lev says, his gaze is blank.

Kaylee's shoulders shake with quiet sobs and the sound cuts me in half. I drop my head into my hands, barely aware of Tony's comforting hand on my shoulder as I feel her shock and loss as if they were my own.

"Hang in there, princess, we're nearly at the end of the story now," Lev says, softly.

"What happened to Gabriel?" Kaylee asks, her voice thick with tears.

"Gabriel was beyond distraught. I think he did love her in his own, perverse way. He tried to give her CPR, bring her back, but I knew it was hopeless. So, I picked up his gun and shot him in the head, watched as his brains splattered on the opposite wall. Watched *his* blood seep across the floor. An eye for an eye, isn't that what they say?"

"An eye for an eye makes the whole world blind," Kaylee murmurs.

Lev looks at her in surprise. "Mahatma Ghandi," he says, looking impressed. "Much as I admired his teachings, he never met Gabriel and he never moved in the kind of circles I did."

"So, what happened after you killed Gabriel?"

"I called Gabriel's men. It wasn't hard for them to believe that Gabriel had shot his wife in a fit of anger and then put a bullet in his own head. They knew how obsessive he was with her, with everything. It helped that I had the medical examiner in my pocket and his findings were in line with my story."

"So, you took over Gabriel's empire. How...convenient," Kaylee's voice is loaded with sarcasm.

"I lost part of myself the day your mother died, Kaylee. She was the only pure thing in my life, the one person who made me feel that maybe, just maybe, I could have a future with her away from it all. I should have run with her that night when she asked me to. Hindsight is a cruel bitch."

"Now I understand why she ran," Kaylee murmurs. "She ran because she was pregnant with me."

"Yes," Lev says. "It was common knowledge that Gabriel couldn't father a child, so she knew she couldn't stay once she discovered she was pregnant. I think she always knew she'd be found from the moment she left, but she just needed enough time to carry you, give birth to you. She must have already found you a new home by the time I caught up with her. I imagine giving you up was the hardest thing she ever did but I know she made that sacrifice to give you the life you deserved, safe from the world she married into. And no one would ever have known. I would never have known."

"Until now," Kaylee whispers. "But, I still don't understand why she put your name on the birth certificate if she was trying to protect me."

Lev shrugs. "Maybe it was in the hope that I would follow her, that we would be a family. Or maybe it was a way of acknowledging me as your father, of reminding herself that you were born out of love, the one good thing that came out of the whole sorry situation. I guess we'll never know for sure."

"No, I guess not," Kaylee says, sadly.

"So, there you have it. The story you wanted to hear. Not exactly a fairy-tale."

"I knew it didn't have a happy ending when I came here, Lev, but what makes it even more heart-breaking is that she could have been your salvation, you could have been each other's salvation," Kaylee says. "Your whole future together hinged on one crucial decision, and the moment you chose not to go with her, you lost any hope of a happy ending. Love isn't always about making the decision that's right for you, it's about what's right for the other person. I know, because I've fallen in love with the most amazing man and I'd follow him anywhere, if he asked me to. I'd risk everything to have a single day with him than live a lifetime without him."

I turn my head away for a minute to hide the wetness in my eyes at Kaylee's words, knowing that I would follow her anywhere too. Wouldn't matter where, so long as we were together.

"You're right," Lev says, his eyes thoughtful as he looks at Kaylee. "And not a day goes by when I don't tell myself the same thing, when I don't imagine the kind of life we could've had together. But that's not the path I chose and there's not a fucking thing I can do about it now."

"Except make a different choice this time," Kaylee says, and I immediately see where she's going with this. My woman isn't just a pretty face.

Lev's laugh is genuine, and it changes his face, making him look younger, more carefree. "You are your father's daughter, all right!" he says, and there's a touch of pride in his voice. "And I thought I was good at manipulation!"

"Not manipulation, Lev. Opportunity. As in yours, to make a different choice, one that helps people instead of hurting them."

"And why, pray tell, would I want to break the habits of a lifetime?" Lev asks, raising an eyebrow. "There's a little too much water under the bridge for a man like me to be seeking redemption."

My heart sinks, knowing that she's losing him, that the unguarded Lev we had a brief glimpse of is retreating behind his wall of careless sarcasm.

"Because you were one decision away from a totally different life, a life where we would have been a real family," Kaylee says, softly. "You. Maria. Me. I would've called you daddy and I would never have doubted your love for me, your determination to keep me safe…" Kaylee's voice breaks as she struggles for composure. "Which is why I'm asking you, begging you, to choose differently. To help me keep those other children safe. Because they're all someone's little girl too, just like a part of me will always be your little girl."

Lev is silent for a long time before answering.

"Come back tomorrow and I'll tell you what you want to know."

Kaylee looks pale and exhausted when we arrive home an hour later. I close the door behind us and pull her into a bear hug, trying to absorb some of her pain. "I've got you, baby," I whisper, as she collapses in my arms, sobbing.

The emotion that spills from her is raw, the pain coming from a place deep inside as she mourns the loss of the parents she knew and the mother she never had the chance to. She's been through so much in such a short space of time, her whole world turned upside-down, and she's dealt with it all with a maturity beyond her years, despite what she may think.

I lift her, carrying her to the sofa and sinking down with her in my lap, stroking her hair, smoothing my hands down her back, comforting her as best I can as her grief continues to pour from her. Finally, her tears begin to slow, her breathing gradually returning to normal as she nuzzles her face into my neck.

"I nearly broke down myself when you told Lev you'd follow me anywhere, trade a whole lifetime for one day together," I murmur, my lips in her hair.

"I meant it," Kaylee says, looking up at me with red-rimmed eyes, her voice husky from crying. "My feelings for you are…impossible to put into simple words."

"I love you, too," I smile, bending to place a kiss on her lips.

"It's just all so tragic," Kaylee says, "how one wrong decision can change the direction of your life, other people's lives. It's like ripples on the water, you never quite realize how far-reaching they are."

"Lev made his choices and he's living with them now," I say. "Despite all the bad shit he's done, I do believe he really loved your mother. He just waited too long to find a way to make their worlds coexist."

"I don't know that I could've done what she did," Kaylee murmurs. "If I was carrying your child, I don't think I'd ever be strong enough, unselfish enough, to give it up."

The thought of Kaylee carrying our baby makes me want to roar and beat my chest. "You'll never be in a position that you have to," I say, my voice full of emotion as I slide my hand over her flat stomach, imagining her swollen with our child.

"One day, I'd really like to make a baby with you," she whispers, her blue eyes searching mine.

"One day, it'll be an enormous pleasure to put our child inside you," I smile, my eyes loving her.

Kaylee pulls my mouth to hers for a lingering kiss, her hands threading through my hair and holding me to her. It's a kiss beyond desire or passion, conveying an emotion deeper than words.

"How does a hot bath, followed by a cold beer and pizza sound?" I ask, nibbling at her mouth.

"Like bliss," she sighs.

"Coming right up."

An hour later, we're sprawled out on the sofa, having eaten our body weight in pizza.

"Do you really think Lev is going to be true to his word tomorrow?" Kaylee asks, sleepily, her hand tracing patterns on my chest under my t-shirt.

"Yeah, I do. I think you got to him there at the end, made him realize how he would have felt if someone had ever tried to hurt his child, hurt you."

"So, what happens once this is all done? With us, I mean?" Kaylee asks, craning her head back to look at me

"What do you mean, with us?" I ask, frowning.

"I mean, I'll have to go back to Bakersfield. My life is there."

"Is it?" I ask, softly, tracing my fingers lightly over her cheek. "Seems to me your life is here now. With me."

"Are you asking me stay?" she breathes.

"No," I reply, and her face drops. "I'm asking you to move in with me."

"Really?" Her eyes nearly pop out of her head. "But…"

"You and I have been through more in the last five days than most people experience in five years," I interrupt, already knowing what she's going to say. "There are some things you just know, and one of those things is that you and I are meant to be together. I'm not letting you go now I've found you again."

Kaylee flings her arms around my neck, hugging me tightly. She pulls back suddenly, looking worried.

"What's up?" I ask, concerned.

"I've still got so much to sort out," she says, her voice edged with panic. "The house, the accountancy business paperwork still to be finalised with the lawyers, and I have to talk to…"

I put my finger against her mouth. "Not you anymore," I say, bending to kiss her softly. "*We*."

KAYLEE

I wake the next morning, missing the warmth of Dawson's body wrapped around mine. Reaching out, I find empty space and my eyes pop open, wondering where he is before I see the note on the pillow next to me.

Gone to the station with Tony. Didn't want to wake you. Back in time to take you to the prison. Love you. Dawson.

I smile as I read his words, already missing him and wondering how long he's been gone. I glance at the clock, surprised to see it's almost midday. I must have been dead to the world because I didn't even hear Dawson leave the house.

I get up and take a quick shower, grimacing as I rifle through my rucksack to see I'm out of clean clothes. I dress in the jeans and shirt I wore yesterday, having only worn them for the few hours we were at the prison, before heading downstairs to do some laundry.

Half an hour later, I'm sitting at the table eating toast and sipping coffee, the only sound the hum of the washing machine in the background.

I can't believe how quickly things are moving between Dawson and I, and a niggle of doubt creeps in. He's been in relationships before, but this is a first for me, and I'm not sure of all the rules, how it's all supposed to work. Aren't you supposed to date for a while before moving in together? I know that being with him, living with him is what I want, to go to sleep and wake up in his arms every day seems like a dream come true, but is that what he really wants? Will he still want that when this is all over, when life goes back to normal? Whatever normal means now.

A knock at the door pulls me from my thoughts, and I frown, wondering who it could be, thinking maybe Dawson left in a hurry and forgot his house key.

I cross to the door, cracking it open to check who it is but before I even have chance to look, the door is shoved forcefully from the other side, sending me crashing backward. I yelp in pain as my head bounces off the bottom tread of the staircase, the yelp turning into a muffled scream as a hand clamps over my mouth and I feel a sharp pinch on my arm. I look down to see a needle sticking out of the skin just above my elbow as a man looms above me, his face oddly familiar.

"What have you…?"

"Don't worry, Maria, just a little something to make you sleep," the man says, smiling at me.

"Ma...Maria?" My tongue suddenly feels thick, my mouth dry, and the world is swirling around me. Belatedly, I try to get up, but there's no strength in my limbs, my body refusing to obey the commands of my brain. "Who...are...you?" I ask, trying to cling to consciousness. My head feels as if it's too heavy for my neck as my eyes start to droop closed.

"It's me, my love. It's John," the man says, making no sense, his voice coming from a million miles away. "I knew we'd find each other again."

The pain in my head is everywhere and it feels as if my skull is cracking open. There's a metallic taste in my mouth and I lick my parched lips, trying to moisten them. I grimace as my tongue hits a tender spot. Did I bite my lip? I can't remember.

Peeling my eyes open, I groan as the light hits them, nausea roiling in my stomach as my vision sways and blurs in front of me. There's a gritty texture under my cheek and I'm suddenly aware that I'm lying on the ground on my side, my face resting on the hard-packed earth beneath me.

As my eyes adjust, I can see I'm in what appears to be an abandoned barn, the light that initially dazzled me coming from various tears in the roof structure where the elements have won the battle with the aged wood. I can vaguely make out a second level, a hayloft, which has also seen better days, the ladder leading up to it warped and rotten.

"Welcome back, Maria."

The voice comes from behind me and I gingerly roll myself over, regretting the movement instantly as pain lances through my head, my eyes struggling to focus on the man sitting in a chair not ten feet from where I'm lying. He looks to be in his mid-fifties, his dark blonde hair liberally sprinkled with grey. Although there's nothing particularly remarkable about him, there's a familiarity to his face that pulls at my memory.

"Sorry about the headache, my love," he says, leaning forward in the chair. "One of the side-effects of the drugs that I never could quite solve, I'm afraid."

"What did you give me?" I croak, struggling to wrap my tongue around the words. I have no idea how much time has passed since he stuck me with the needle. It could be hours, or days, and we could be anywhere by now.

"Ah, yes. It's one of my own, a clever blend of central nervous system depressants with an inhibitor to prevent cardiovascular collapse. I couldn't risk you dying on me...not yet, not until we're all here," he says, smiling as if we're discussing the weather. "Remember how you used to come to me for sedatives when you couldn't sleep? I used to make them especially for you, just the right dosage to help you bear the burden of the life you married into with Gabriel. You deserved only the very best, my love, and it was always a pleasure to provide it for you."

"You knew Gabriel?"

He frowns. "You're a little confused but the effects will wear off soon. I must confess, sometimes it feels surreal to me too, working for Gabriel for all those years," he says, his eyes glazing over as he loses himself in memories.

"You manufactured drugs for Gabriel!" I say, pushing myself into a sitting position and waiting for the room to right itself again.

"It's all coming back now isn't it, my darling?" John says. "Gabriel gave me the opportunity to utilize my skills, unlock the potential of so many drugs without the usual legal constraints. It was like being let loose in the chemical equivalent of a candy store, only instead of candy it was stimulants, opiates, hallucinogens, sedatives," he says, and a rabid enthusiasm replaces his previously glazed look.

I feel like I've drifted into a chemistry lesson, my addled brain still under the influence of whatever drug it was he told me he'd injected me with. My brain may be fuzzy, but one thing is perfectly clear - the man is completely bat-shit crazy.

"You've made a mistake. I'm not Maria. My name is Kaylee and I have no idea who you are." That's not strictly true as that sense of familiarity is tickling the back of my brain again, trying to place where I've seen him before.

"I don't make mistakes!" he shrieks, leaping from his chair, his face mottled with rage. He bangs his clenched fists violently against his head, pulling at his hair and I shrink back against the barn wall, my hands scrabbling in the dirt behind me, trying to find something, anything, I can use as a weapon.

Seems he's not bat-shit crazy after all. He's a total psychopath.

John paces, muttering under his breath. "Kaylee? Yes, yes, that's right! There was a little girl called Mikhaila...but she...what happened to her?" he asks himself. He takes a deep breath and his expression clears, the rage evaporating as quickly as it appeared.

"I... I'm sorry...um...John?" I stutter, vaguely remembering him saying the name before I passed out. "I didn't mean to upset you."

"It's okay, Maria," John sighs. "I love you too much to stay mad at you for long."

"You loved my moth...me?" I ask, deciding it may be safer to play along, not wanting to enrage him again. My fingers close around a small metal object and I claw at the dirt behind me, trying to loosen it.

"I've always loved you, Maria. More than Gabriel, who was possessive and cruel, or Lev, who put his own agenda above your safety. But not me. No, I risked everything to keep you safe!" he shouts, spittle flying from his mouth. "I covered your tracks, made sure you had everything you needed during your pregnancy, even helped with Mikhaila."

"Who's Mikhaila?" I ask, as he mentions the name for a second time.

"Your daughter, my love. You wanted her name to reflect her Russian heritage, remember?" he says, his anger dissipating again. "She was Lev's child, but he wasn't there for her. I was. We could have been a family, just the three of us, but it's too late now."

"It not too late, we can still be a family," I whisper. "We can leave now, go and get Mikhaila, go wherever we want," I say, knowing that if I can get him outside, there's a chance I can make a run for it.

John suddenly moves toward me, bending down to cup my face in his hands. "I'd do anything for you, Maria," he murmurs, and my heart stutters at the sheer madness in his eyes. "I've waited so long to hear you say those words, that we can be together again. Make me the happiest man alive and tell me you love me, like you did the night you came to me for help. The night we made love."

"The night we…?" Oh God! My mother slept with this man? Had she really loved him? Or had she used him to help her escape Gabriel?

I freeze as his face moves to within inches of mine and I whimper as his hands dig painfully into my scalp, grabbing fistfuls of my hair as he grinds his lips against mine.

Clutching the metal object I've unearthed in my hand, I swing my arm, stabbing the nail into the side of his neck. He yells in surprise and pain, falling backward, his hand flying to his neck as blood trickles down into the collar of his shirt.

Instantly, I'm on my feet, sprinting for the door on the other side of the barn, my heart almost choking me as I pray that it's open. It seems to take an eternity to reach it and my worst fears are realized as it refuses to yield under the weight of my body as I crash into it. There's a plank of wood holding it closed and my breath escapes in sobs as I try to lift it, clawing at the wood and drawing blood as the rough surface tears into the flesh of my fingers.

I spin, pressing my back against the door, frantically looking for another escape route as John advances on me, pulling the nail from his neck. He's bleeding but the damage appears to be superficial and my plan to buy myself enough time to escape crumbles around me.

"Why did you do that, Maria? You have to stop running now," he rasps, his face dark with anger again. "You know it's not good for you or the baby."

"B..baby?" I stammer. The man is lost in another time, another place, living out some twisted fantasy.

He stops in front of me, reaching out to touch my face and I turn my head, sinking my teeth into his hand, almost vomiting as his blood spurts into my mouth. He curses loudly, lashing out with his other arm as he backhands me and my head smacks against the door behind me. Pain explodes along my cheek and I lean forward, giving into the urge to vomit as I retch onto the earth at my feet before collapsing to the floor.

"You don't want us to be a family at all! You're lying to me again, Maria!" he shouts. "You know what happened the last time you lied to me!" He lunges at me, grabbing me by the hair and dragging me toward the chair he occupied earlier. He shoves me down in the seat roughly, yanking my arms behind me, holding my wrists in a bruising grip as he secures them with tape.

"I didn't want to hurt you, Maria, but this only ends one way now. No more pain, no more suffering, just you and me, together forever, because If I can't have you, no one can! There's just one person missing but if they've followed my instructions, Lev should be on his way now."

"You're insane!" I sob. "Lev is in prison!"

"Shhh! It's okay. I know this is hard for you, my love, but it's all for the best, you'll see," he says, moving around to crouch in front of me. He lifts his hand to brush the hair away from my face and I jerk away from his touch. His hand moves down, wrapping around my neck. "You are so beautiful," he whispers. "Just as beautiful as I remember."

I squeeze my eyes shut, whimpering as his hand continues its downward journey, skimming over my breasts toward my stomach, the sound of his ragged breathing making the bile rise in my throat again.

"You...you need...to stop," I stammer, trying to keep my voice steady. "I'm not f...feeling well and we don't want to hurt the b... baby."

He frowns. "You're right, my love. I'm sorry. I'd never hurt you or the baby," he says, and I release a shaky breath as he stands up, looking at the watch strapped to his wrist. "I really thought they'd be here by now. My note was clear enough."

"Note?"

"Telling them where to find us," he says patiently, as if explaining something to a five-year old. "If the mountain can't get to Muhammad, then Muhammad must come to the mountain," he smiles, and I'm pretty sure he's twisted that proverb to suit his needs.

"Why do you need Lev here?" I ask.

"So that I can finish this, once and for all. Getting access to him by infiltrating the prison was proving much harder than I imagined, but when I saw you the other night, I knew it was the sign I'd been waiting for. God sent you back to me and I knew what I had to do, what He wanted me to do!"

John voice is full of wonder. "When Lev arrives, none of us will be leaving here, Maria. I'm going to end this once and for all, penance for our sins, all part of God's plan."

I stare at him in horror, the memory that's been tickling away at the back of my brain suddenly coming into sharp focus as I remember where I've seen John before.

He's the guard from the prison.

He thinks I'm Maria.

And he's going to kill us all.

DAWSON

The last few hours have been the worst of my life. Coming back to the house to find Kaylee gone, blood on the stairs and the note pinned to inside of the front door has left me all kinds of fucked up.

Why the hell did I agree go to the station to meet Tony? If I'd just ignored his call, stayed in bed with Kaylee's warm body wrapped around mine, she'd still be safe, not in the hands of a fucking mad man bent on his own warped version of revenge. The thought of what he might have already done to her has me grinding my teeth in frustration and I know I'll tear the whole fucking world apart to find her if I have to.

"How you holding up, champ?" Tony says, glancing across at me as we make our way to the prison.

I shake my head, staring blankly out of the car window, no amount of words able to express the shit that's going on in my mind. Angry, scared and helpless don't even come close.

"We're gonna get her back, Dawson. If it's the last fucking thing I ever do, you hear me?" Tony says, his voice full of cold determination.

"I get to talk to Lev," I say, pinning Tony with a look that would intimidate a lesser man.

Tony sighs, "Okay, but you've got to keep it under control, Dawson. Going in there all guns blazing isn't going to get Kaylee back."

"I know that, Tony! More than anyone! You're the one who brought this whole fucking thing to my door, who promised me nothing would happen to her!" I know I'm being out of order as soon as the words leave my mouth, but I'm hurting and looking for someone to take it out on.

"You're not telling me anything I haven't told myself a hundred times in the last few hours," Tony says, quietly.

I sigh, letting my head drop back against the headrest. "That was out of order. I'm sorry. Truth is, I'm pissed at myself more than anyone else. I should've tried harder to talk her out of it."

"She's a grown woman, Dawson. What were you gonna do? Lock her up, forbid her to leave the house? You know, as well as I do, how determined she was to see Lev, with or without my help."

"I know," I sigh. "And I also know that, right now, I'd do anything to swap places with her."

All we need to do now, is convince Lev to do that very same thing.

I keep looking at the door on the opposite side of the glass, waiting for the guard to bring Lev into the visitor's area. Every minute that passes is another minute that Kaylee's life is in danger, and my feelings of helplessness and frustration increase as I wait.

After what seems like an eternity, the door opens, and Lev is led into the room by the guard. The door shuts with a clunk and a red light appears over the top to indicate the room has been locked down, the signal for the guard to remove Lev's handcuffs.

If he's surprised to see me, he doesn't show it, his expression one of mild interest as he sits down on the stool and picks up the phone, waiting for me to do the same.

"I hope there's a good reason you're here instead of my daughter," Lev says, quirking an eyebrow.

"I'm Detective Dawson Ford. I'm a…friend of Kaylee's."

"Is that so?" Lev replies. "And what can I do for you Detective Dawson Ford, *friend* of Kaylee's?"

"Kaylee is missing," I say, getting straight to the point.

Lev's eyes fly to mine, narrowing, as if waiting for the punchline. "When you say missing…"

"Missing as in abducted," I say, bluntly.

"Who the hell would want to abduct her?" Lev explodes.

"A man who only resurfaced recently, strangely enough when you were transferred to Stanislaus," I reply. "He's been working here as a guard, using a fake ID that was so well done even we found it hard to trace it back to him. Why would someone go to all that trouble to get a job at the prison where you're being detained?" I ask.

"Well, that very much depends on who the fuck it is you're referring to?" Lev growls.

"A man called John Grayson," I say, watching Lev carefully.

"John Grayson? Are you fucking kidding me? That man was nuttier than squirrel shit!" Lev says, with a look of disbelief.

"So, you know him?"

"*Knew* him," Lev corrects. "Haven't heard his name for years. Didn't know the guy that well, tended to keep my distance when he worked for Gabriel."

"He worked for Gabriel too?"

"For years," Lev replies. "The man was an unstable genius who cooked up all manner of fucking weird chemical shit. Spent far too much time in his lab self-experimenting with his own inventions, if you ask me. Made him more than a little cray-cray," he says, spinning his finger next to his temple.

"Shit!" I curse, my fears for Kaylee increasing tenfold.

Lev looks at me closely, sitting forward on his stool. "There's more, isn't there? What are you not telling me Detective Ford?"

"Grayson's note said that he has Maria."

"Maria? But she's...shit! The fucking fruit loop thinks Kaylee is Maria!" Lev says, rubbing his free hand over his eyes and it's the first time I've seen him genuinely upset. "What on earth would John want with Maria? Unless…"

"Unless John Grayson was the man who helped Maria escape from Gabriel," I finish.

"Jesus!" Lev breathes.

"He must have seen Kaylee when she came here the other night and thought she was Maria," I say.

"The other night?"

"Kaylee came here demanding to see you. Caused a disturbance. I was the one who answered the call."

"She did that?" Lev asks in surprise.

I nod. "She wanted to meet her birth father, despite all the things she'd read and heard about you. What I don't understand, though, is why would Grayson help Maria? What reason could he possibly have had for risking his position with Gabriel?"

"There's only one reason a man is prepared to risk everything, including his own life," Lev says, looking at me.

"Love," I say, thinking of Kaylee. "He was in love with her."

"What does he want? Money?" Lev asks.

"He's not interested in money."

"Then what the fuck does he want?"

"You. In exchange for Kaylee."

"What the hell does he want with me?" Lev asks, and it's clear he really doesn't have a clue.

"That's the part we were hoping you could help us with. The note he left had the coordinates of where to find them, a derelict barn about twenty miles from here. His instructions were specific, that we're to take you to him and once he has you, he'll release Kaylee. If anyone other than you attempts to go in...he'll send her out...one piece at a time," I say, forcing out the last few words.

"He's bluffing," Lev says. "Why would he give up his leverage by harming her? That's suicide. Even if I agree to it, there's no guarantee he'll release her."

"*If* you agree to it? Are you fucking kidding me? You don't have a choice! If Grayson is as unhinged as you claim, he's capable of anything!" I explode, trying to get a grip on my anger.

"Easy, tiger. I can practically feel the testosterone rolling off you from here." Lev looks at me closely and realization suddenly dawns on his face. "You're the man she was talking about yesterday, the one she said she'd follow anywhere!" he says. "Well, well, my girl has only gone and fallen in love with a cop. How...cliché. Shame you weren't doing your job when she needed you earlier."

A red mist descends in front of my eyes as Lev hits a nerve. "Are you really going to do this now, Lev? Because I really don't have time for your fucking mind games! This is your daughter, your flesh and blood, being held by a man who's capable of God only knows what! Who knows what he's already done to her, what he's doing to her right now while I'm sitting here having this pointless fucking conversation with you?" I'm shouting now, any attempt to keep my shit together long gone.

"You're turning this into a pissing competition, just like you do with everything else. This is about saving a life, your daughter's life. What's it going to take for you to put someone above yourself for once in your lousy fucking life?" I demand. "You want me to get down on my knees and beg? Because if that's what it takes, I will. I'll hate every fucking second of it, but I'll do it. For her," I say, breathing hard. "What are *you* prepared to do for her, Lev?"

Lev looks at me for a long time, his face unreadable. "You finished?"

"Yeah, I'm finished," I say, defeated, knowing I lost any chance of persuading Lev to help when I lost my temper.

"Good. When do we leave?"

An hour later, we turn off the highway, following an old dirt track for about a mile until the abandoned barn comes into view. It's an isolated spot with nothing but fields stretching in all directions and the only sign that anyone else is here is the black BMW with rental plates parked at the back of the old building.

Lev is in the back seat, still in handcuffs, but the prison uniform has been replaced by a pair of jeans, a button-down shirt and jacket with a bulletproof vest underneath. One of the buttons on the jacket is actually a cleverly disguised surveillance device which will allow us to see and hear everything that happens once Lev is inside the barn.

"Are you sure he won't know Lev is wearing a wire?" I ask Tony, as he parks the car a good distance from the barn.

"Wire is outdated term, a throwback to when UC cops had a ten-pound device strapped to their groin," Tony says. "Nowadays it's a digital surveillance device, and this one is smaller than a pack of gum. It'll transmit a signal back to my cell phone and it's good for about four hours recording time."

"Let's hope this is all over long before that," I say, heavily.

"It will be, champ," Tony says, slapping my shoulder.

"Aw, look at you two," Lev says from the backseat. "Shall I leave? Give you two a little privacy? Does Kaylee know?" Lev says, in a mock whisper, moving his finger back and forth between myself and Tony.

"Glad you're finding this so fucking funny, Lev," Tony says, glaring at the other man.

"Particularly when your daughter's life is in your hands."

"Believe me, there's not a single fucking thing about this I find funny," Lev says, all the humor leaving his face. "I'm putting my life on the line for a woman I've only met twice, daughter or not."

I swear to God, I want to punch him in his fucking face until it doesn't resemble a face anymore!

"You're clear on the plan?" Tony continues, his mouth a grim line as he resists the same violent urges I'm feeling.

"Yes, I'm clear," Lev replies, sighing impatiently. "I go into the barn. Kaylee comes out of the barn. You send in the four units that are waiting with baited breath for your signal. They swoop in and save the day, along with my ass. Simple."

It does sound as simple as Lev says, despite his sarcasm, but my heart is beating me to death at the thought of all the ways that plan could go wrong.

"Right, we're ready then," Tony says, and we all get out of the car, Tony walking round to Lev to unlock his cuffs.

Lev rubs his wrists, taking in a deep lungful of air. "Ah, the sweet smell of freedom. With a subtle hint of cow shit, if I'm not mistaken," he smiles. "Oh, how I've missed those smells!"

"Get Kaylee out of there alive, and I'll personally have a truckload of cow shit delivered to your cell," I say, with a false smile.

"Better that than the smell of human excrement that pervades the place," Lev says with a grimace.

"I'm sure we can talk shit when this is all over," Tony says, drily. "Your device is good for five meters," he says, looking at Lev. "Any further away than that and we'll lose signal, so try to stay as close to Grayson as you can."

"Aye, aye, skipper!" Lev says, saluting Tony.

"Right. Let's get this done," Tony sighs.

"Later, boys," Lev says, lifting a hand and sauntering toward the barn, looking for all the world as if he's just out for a stroll in the countryside.

Tony and I climb back into the car and Tony connects his cell phone to a special app which will stream the picture from Lev's device.

I watch Lev as he reaches the barn, but instead of going to the door, he makes a turn and starts walking around the other side of the old building.

"What the fuck is he doing?" I explode.

"Don't panic, boys," Lev's voice is low as it reaches us through the cell phone at the same time the picture kicks in. "Just having a little reccy to get the lay of the land, see if there are any other exits. Always good to know your escape routes."

I release the breath I was holding, a little more reassured that Lev isn't about to do a runner as he circles back around to the front of the barn. Tony and I watch on the screen as he reaches the door, pushing it open cautiously, before stepping inside.

It takes a moment for the camera to adjust to the lower light level but when it does, we can make out the outline of someone sitting in a chair. Lev moves forward, and the person comes into focus, my heart stuttering as I see it's Kaylee.

"Fuck!" I shout. "Look what that fucking bastard's done to her!"

She's tied to the chair, her mouth covered with tape and her hair is matted with blood on one side. There's a red welt across her cheek, as if she's been struck across the face, but it's the look of sheer terror in her eyes that almost has me out of the car and heading for the barn, ready to commit murder with my bare hands.

"Don't, Dawson!" Tony says, putting a restraining hand on the arm I didn't realize was reaching for the car door. "You go in there now, and this is all over."

A movement outside the barn catches our attention and we see Lev reappear. He removes his jacket and takes off his bulletproof vest, pulling the surveillance device out and holding it up to his face.

"Sorry, boys. Just following John's instructions," he says, dropping the device to the ground and crushing it under his shoe before turning and disappearing back inside the barn.

"Shit!" Tony shouts, slamming his palm against the steering wheel.

Our plan is already falling apart around us, and to make matters worse, we're now fighting blind and totally reliant on Lev Sarado.

Kaylee

I watch as John removes the heavy plank of wood holding the door closed, feeling a little better that I couldn't move it earlier as even he's struggling under its weight. He's cleaned and dressed the wounds on his neck and hand and I feel a sense of satisfaction knowing that I inflicted them.

After my attempted escape earlier, John wasn't taking any chances and in addition to the tape binding my wrists, I now also have tape covering my mouth and wrapped around my legs. My arms are beginning to cramp from being in one position for so long and I wiggle my fingers a little to ease the pain.

I feel as if I've been here for days, and the only thing keeping me going is the thought of seeing Dawson again, of being wrapped in the warmth and safety of his arms.

My head whips up at the sound of footsteps outside and my eyes round in shock as I see Lev enter the barn. He walks cautiously toward me, his eyes still adjusting to the gloom. When he gets close enough to see it's me, he brings his index finger to his lips, silently telling me to remain quiet. I shake my head, trying to warn him with my eyes, unable to speak through the tape covering my mouth.

"The great Lev Sarado! You made it!"

John's cheerful voice reaches us as he emerges from the shadows at the corner of the barn and my heart stops as I see he's holding a gun.

"John!" Lev says, turning to look at the other man. "Good to see you again!"

The two men sound like old friends meeting up for a beer rather than two men who are more than capable of killing each other.

"I need you to do something for me, Lev," John says, as if he's casually asking for a favor. "Go back outside and take off the jacket and vest, remove the surveillance device and destroy it. Make sure the two cops out there know what you've done."

My heart skips as John mentions the two cops, sure that Dawson is one of them, and no doubt Tony is the other.

"I don't know what device you're talking about, John," Lev says, innocently.

"Oh, come now, Lev," John smiles. "You know you'll go to hell if you tell lies."

"Must have missed the memo on that one," Lev says. "Guess hell is gonna have a special torture chamber just for me."

"Please do as I ask, Lev, or I'll start by shooting off one of her fingers and I'm sure I don't need to tell you what it feels like to lose a finger," he grins.

"Do that and you'll lose any bargaining power you had with me," Lev threatens.

"It may have escaped your notice, but you lost any power you had the second you walked in here," John says coldly.

A flash of frustration passes across Lev's eyes and I hold my breath, thinking he's going to refuse John's instructions. After several long seconds, he sighs heavily, turning to walk back out of the barn. A minute later, his voice reaches us from outside the open door.

"Sorry, boys. Just following John's instructions."

I close my eyes, my heart aching as a tear slips down my cheek, knowing that one of the people he's talking to is Dawson. It's almost as if I can feel his proximity and the yearning to see him almost chokes me.

Lev strolls back into the barn, the jacket and vest he was wearing earlier now gone. He comes to a halt a few feet in front of my chair and turns to look at John. "It was you who helped Maria when she left Gabriel, wasn't it?" he asks.

John smiles. "Yes. She came to me the same night you refused to help her. I loved her from the moment I laid eyes on her, spent five long years waiting for her to notice me in return, and when she finally did, I knew I would do anything for her. Unlike you!" John accuses, his voice full of condemnation. "You wanted things to stay as they were even though you knew how Gabriel treated her, why she needed those sedatives I used to make for her. You have no idea what it's like to put someone else's needs above your own!"

"You're right, John," Lev says, and there's genuine pain in his voice that surprises me. "I should have left with Maria that night, run as fast and as far away as we could. I should have put my faith in her, in what we felt for each other. Because I did love her, despite what you or anyone else may think. I just didn't love her enough, but I'll be forever grateful that you did, because at least you gave her the chance I never could, gave her a safe place to have our child."

"You should be on your fucking knees thanking me, because without me Mikhaila would never have been born!"

"Mikhaila? You mean Kaylee?" Lev looks shocked. "She called you Mikhaila!" he whispers, turning to look at me with something like pride in his eyes, "after my father Mikhailo!"

"I was there that day, waiting for you," John says.

"It was you who tipped Gabriel off!" Lev realizes.

"Yes, and it was me who left the trail for you to find Maria," John replies. "Didn't you ever wonder why it was so easy after all those months of searching? It was because I wanted you to find her, you and Gabriel. I knew the only way Maria, Mikhaila and I could be a family was if you were both removed from the equation. I loved that little girl as if she were my own. I watched her sleeping while I waited for you to arrive. Maria didn't even know I was there."

"Mikhaila was there? But I thought…" Lev looks distraught.

"You thought what? That Maria would give up her own daughter?" John says, with disgust. "You never knew her at all! She loved that child more than her own life, never had any intention of giving her up. She was prepared to run forever if it meant she could keep her child, and I had every intention of helping her do that if it meant I could be with them. The kind of love she had for Mikhaila, the sacrifices she was prepared to make, are the kind of selfless emotions you'll never understand!"

Fresh tears spill down my cheeks knowing my mother never had any intention of giving me up. She loved me, more than anything and my heart breaks all over again knowing how her story ended.

John's mouth curls in disgust as he looks at Lev. "When you arrived, I had to listen to you to putting your filthy hands on Maria, but it was a sacrifice I was prepared to make, knowing that Gabriel was on his way, that he would kill you when he found you together."

"You were always the bigger threat, Lev. The plan was to use Gabriel to remove you from the picture, which only left Gabriel for me to take care of, and I had a special concoction all ready for him. It should have all been so simple, but something went wrong and...I can't..." John's words trail off, his brow furrowing as if searching for a deeply buried memory.

"What went wrong was you forgot to let Maria in on your little plan!" Lev shouts angrily. "You didn't account for the fact that she would sacrifice her own life to save mine, you stupid fucking fool! If you had she'd still be alive! Her death is on *you*, John! Not me, you! You may as well have just pulled the fucking trigger yourself!"

"No, no, no, no!" John moans, clutching his head. "She's not dead! She's right there!" he yells, swinging the gun in my direction. "She came back to me! God has given us a second chance!"

"No, He hasn't, John," Lev says, his voice dropping to a growl. "God doesn't give people like us second chances!"

"Shut up! Shut the fuck up! Move back!" John shouts, pointing the gun at Lev.

Lev obeys reluctantly, moving back a few paces behind me and I watch as John walks toward me, coming to a halt just in front of the chair.

"Slide the gun to me, Lev," he says.

"Gun?" Lev frowns.

"The one you slipped into your boot when you took a little walk around the barn earlier. A little something left by one of your informants? Did you really think I wouldn't notice? Now, slide the fucking gun toward me, or I'll blow her fingers off, one by one," John snarls, pointing the gun at my hand.

"I've gone along with your little game up 'til now John, but I know you won't hurt Mikhaila," Lev says, watching John carefully.

"Mikhaila? I think you're a little confused, Lev," John frowns.

"I think you're the one confused," Lev replies. "Actually, scratch that. You're crazier than a box of frogs on a barbecue. Take a good, hard look at the woman in this chair, John," he says, sweeping his arm toward me. "What color were Maria's eyes?"

"H…her eyes?" John stutters. "They were brown, a beautiful, deep brown,"

"Then why does the woman you have tied to that chair have blue eyes, John? The exact same shade as mine! Where is the mole that Maria had just above her lip, the tiny scar by her left eye?" Lev continues, knowing he's getting under John's skin.

Lev's goading makes me nervous, especially as John has a gun pointed at me, and I know how quickly he can flip from relatively sane to completely unhinged, how easy it would be for him to just squeeze the trigger.

"Look at her, John. What are you scared of? The truth? Look at her, goddammit!" Lev shouts.

John's eyes flicker over my face, uncertainty clouding his expression as he looks at me, a battle warring behind his eyes as he sees the differences Lev has pointed out.

"No! It's not true. It's Maria...I…"

"It's not Maria, John!" Lev yells, pushing him, poking him like a bull-fighter trying to enrage a bull. "Maria is dead! She's been dead for twenty years! Shot in the heart by Gabriel because *you* put her in harm's way!"

"NOOOOO!" John screams, his eyes rolling wildly as he tries to deny Lev's words, his hands going to his head and tearing at his scalp as if he's trying to rip the memories from his mind.

"No, no, he's lying, he's a liar, it's what he does," he mutters to himself.

He paces in agitation in front of my chair, and Lev takes his opportunity, launching himself at the other man and tackling him to the ground, pinning him with one arm across his throat.

I force a scream around the tape covering my mouth, trying to warn Lev as I see John lift the gun toward his head. Lev's free hand flies up to block him, grasping John's wrist and the gun wavers back and forth as the two men tussle in a deadly arm wrestle.

"None of us are getting out of here alive, Lev," John grunts, a demented look in his eyes as sweat pops out on his brow. "This is how God wants it to end, how it was meant to end."

The sound of the gun discharging echoes around the old barn. I scream again as pain explodes in my left arm, looking down in shock to see blood seeping through my shirt, trying to draw breath as the pain becomes all-consuming.

"You just signed your own death warrant!" Lev roars, and with a surge of strength he smashes John's hand to the ground, sending the gun skittering across the earth.

"This doesn't end how *you* want it to, John. This ends how *I* want it to!" he rasps.

I watch in horror as a needle appears in Lev's hand and he stabs it into John's neck, emptying the syringe as he looks straight into the other man's eyes. "There was never anything outside, no gun in my boot, but I did have a little something up my sleeve I brought with me from prison!"

"Wh…what…?" John gasps.

"Potassium chloride," Lev says, "you're not the only one who knows a little something about chemical compounds, and I'm sure I don't need to tell you that, in a matter of minutes, your heart is going to feel like it's trying to burst out of your chest. You're going to piss your pants, John, probably even shit yourself as your body convulses and you writhe in agony until you die. In other words, you're about to have a massive heart attack."

Lev pushes himself away from the other man, leaping to his feet and hurrying over to me. He pulls a penknife from the pocket of his jeans and cuts through the tape that binds my wrists and legs. I barely feel the pain as he rips the tape from my mouth, my mind focused only on the burning throb in my arm.

"Hold tight, princess. I'm getting you out of here," Lev says, and I moan in pain as he scoops me up in his arms, fighting the darkness that's threatening to swallow me, my head lolling against his shoulder as he turns toward the barn door.

I try not to look at John moaning and retching as we pass, trying to block out the sight of the other man writhing on the floor, not wanting to remember the sound of another human being dying, no matter what he's done.

The light almost blinds me as Lev throws open the barn door, but we've barely made it a few paces before a movement over his shoulder catches my eye. Time seems to slow as I see John, foaming at the mouth, his face mottled and his eyes bulging as he reaches for the discarded gun and levels it at us.

I scream Lev's name, but it's too late. John pulls the trigger, collapsing face first into the dirt and a split second later, Lev stumbles, sending us both crashing to the ground. I moan, trying to catch my breath, winded by the weight of Lev's body pinning me down, watching in terror as blood blooms across the front of his shirt.

"No, no, no!" I choke, pressing my uninjured hand against the wound, trying to stem the flow of blood. "Don't you dare! Don't you die on me, Lev!"

Lev lifts a hand to my face. "Shhh, it's okay, princess. It's poetic. I was...wrong. God does give people...like me...second chances." His voice is fading, along with the life in his eyes as he bends, whispering something in my ear before his head drops to the earth beside mine, his gaze empty.

"Noooo!" I scream, trying to cradle his head, crying out as pain burns through my arm.

The sound of running feet reaches me and I close my eyes, sobbing in sheer relief as I hear Dawson shouting my name. Lev's weight is suddenly lifted from me and Dawson's face swims into view above me.

He falls to his knees beside me, gathering me up against him. "I'm here, baby, I'm here!"

I whimper as my arm is jostled with the movement, biting my lip as Dawson pulls back, his eyes searching mine in panic.

"My arm," I moan, looking down to see I'm covered in blood, not sure if it's mine or Lev's.

"The paramedics are here," Tony says breathlessly, joining a pale Dawson at my side.

"Hang on, angel, help is coming."

I'm vaguely aware of the sound of sirens and the next few minutes passes in a blur as the paramedics rush to take care of me, giving me a shot of morphine for the pain. I lose sight of Dawson in the melee of people surrounding me and start to panic, calling his name hysterically as they transfer me to a gurney and move me toward the ambulance.

I sob as his familiar face comes into view above me. "Don't leave me!"

"Never!" Dawson promises, bringing my uninjured hand to his mouth. "Go to sleep, baby. I'll be right here when you wake up."
Reassured, I close my eyes, clinging to his hand as I surrender to the effects of the morphine.

DAWSON

Kaylee screams, and I leap from the chair next to the bed, settling my weight alongside her on the hospital bed and gently gathering her against me.

"Dawson?" Her eyes flicker open and lock onto mine. Her breathing is labored, as if she's been running, a sheen of sweat on her forehead.

"I'm here, sweetheart," I say, bending to kiss her softly, careful of her swollen lip. "Bad dream?"

"Yeah," she gasps. "Are you real?"

I pull her a little closer. "Very real, and not going anywhere. Wanna tell me about the dream?"

"I was back at the barn with Lev, and I thought we'd gotten away, but then I saw John with the gun...and I screamed...I tried to warn Lev...but it was too late. I was too late!" He's dead, isn't he?" she chokes.

I nod. "I'm sorry, baby."

Her face crumples and I pull her closer as tears spill silently down her cheeks. I can feel her loss and trauma and there's something heart-wrenching about the quietness of her grief.

After a few minutes, she takes a steadying breath, nuzzling her face into my neck as she tries to lift her arms around me, wincing as her left arm refuses to move.

"Lie still. You're all bandaged up after surgery," I murmur, kissing her forehead.

"Surgery?"

"To patch up your arm. You've been out for hours. You were lucky. It was a through and through, but they had to repair the muscle damage. It's going to take time and therapy, but you should regain full use of it."

Her eyes are worried. "Should?"

"You *will*," I correct, "because you're a fighter. What you've just survived proves that more than anything."

Her expression is forlorn as she looks at me. "I don't feel like much of a fighter, right now."

"You're exhausted, baby. You've been through a traumatic experience. I should never have left you on your own, should've been there to protect you!" I close my eyes, trying to get control of my own emotions.

She reaches up with her good hand, smoothing the wetness from my eyes with her thumb. "You can't protect me from a threat we didn't know existed," she says, softly. "And it was me that set the whole chain of events in motion the night John saw me at the prison."

What's done is done and we'll get through what comes next together," I say, knowing that blaming ourselves for someone else's actions won't change anything. "What I do know is you are the best thing that's ever come into my life and I went a little crazy when I came home to find you gone."

She gives me a watery smile. "Just a little crazy?"

"Out of my fucking mind!" I growl.

She swallows hard, her eyes clouding over. "Believe me, you'll never compare to John Grayson's kind of crazy,"

Before I can reply, there's a tap at the door and Tony pokes his head in.

"How you doing, angel?" he says, looking relieved to see Kaylee awake.

"Ah, you know, getting kidnapped and shot is all in a day's work," she jokes, weakly.

Tony closes the door and moves into the room, coming to stand at the foot of the bed with his hands in his pockets. "For what it's worth, I'm really sorry. I never meant for..."

"It's not your fault, Tony," Kaylee interrupts. "It was my choice to help and you were upfront with me from the start."

Tony still looks guilty. "Yeah, but kidnapping and shooting were never part of the plan."

"It could have been much worse," Kaylee says, matter-of-factly. "Now, if we're done with the guilt trip, I'd like to give my statement."

"Now?" I ask, looking at her in surprise. "Are you sure? Maybe tomorrow would be better, when you've had chance to rest."

"I need to do it now, Dawson, while it's still fresh," Kaylee says firmly, and I know her mind is made up.

I give her a quick kiss, climbing off the bed and moving toward the chair, knowing that she's going to need a little distance from me to say what she needs to say.

Tony takes the chair next to mine, looking at Kaylee as he pulls out his notepad and pen. "Take your time, angel, and if you need to stop, just say the word."

Kaylee nods, taking a deep breath before she starts to talk. She tells us how John forced his way into the house and injected her with a drug, how she woke up in the barn not knowing how much time had passed.

"It didn't take long to work out that he thought I was Maria. He was lost in another time, his feelings for her were more obsession than love," Kaylee murmurs.

Tony indicates the ugly bruise along her cheek. "What happened to your face?"

"He...uh...tried to kiss me," she says, her gaze shifting to me as I clench my fists. "I stabbed him in the neck with a nail I found on the ground and bit his hand trying to escape. This was my punishment," she says, touching her cheek lightly.

"Did he touch you? Put his hands on you?" I ask, trying to keep my voice steady, dreading the answer but needing to know.

"He... started to, and I think he wanted to…have sex with...with Maria. His mind was trapped in a time when she was still pregnant, so I played along...convinced him that I was sick, and it would hurt the baby. Thankfully, it worked," she whispers, her eyes dropping to her lap.

I drop my head into my hands, pushing my fingers through my hair in agitation. I want to go to her more than anything but know that if I comfort her right now, while she's reliving this, she may always associate my touch with John's.

"He never intended for any of us to get out of there alive," Kaylee continues. "He believed God had sent him a message the night he saw me at the prison, that we all had to pay for our sins, and if it hadn't been for Lev, he would have got his way."

Tony frowns. "How did Lev get hold of the drug he used on Grayson?"

Kaylee shrugs. "He already had it on him. You said it yourself, just because Lev was in jail didn't mean he couldn't still make things happen when he needed to. He fought with John and that's when the gun went off and I got shot. Lev injected John with the drug and cut me loose. We were both so close to getting out," she murmurs.

Tony looks thoughtful. "He came through for you, in the end."

"He did," Kaylee agrees. "And he also came through for you."

"How so?" Tony asks, looking confused.

"He whispered something to me, just before he died. Does Michael Sarandon mean anything to you?" Kaylee asks.

Tony looks surprised. "Michael Sarandon? CEO of MS Corp?"

"If you say so," she smiles. "According to Lev, he's your guy. Bring him down, and the rest will fall, his words not mine."

"You've got to be fucking kidding me!" Tony looks like he's still in shock "He's the last person I would expect to be involved in something as nasty as child trafficking!"

I look across at Tony. "You know what they say, it's always the ones you least expect."

"Ain't that the truth!" Tony agrees. "Okay, well, I'll get your statement prepared for you to sign tomorrow, angel, but if there's anything else you remember in the meantime, just let me know."

"I will," Kaylee smiles at Tony. "And thanks for checking in on me."

"Your thanks is the last thing I deserve," Tony grimaces. "I've been pacing a groove in the corridor out there, waiting to see if you're okay."

"I will be," Kaylee says. "*We* will be," she adds, her eyes loving as she looks across at me.

"I'll leave you in peace, then," Tony says, lifting his hand in farewell before heading out the door.

"I need to shower," Kaylee says, the second the door closes. "Can you help me?"

I nod, understanding her need to get clean, helping her out of the hospital bed and into the bathroom. I untie her hospital gown, easing her out of it and watch as she removes her panties. I grit my teeth as I see the marks and bruises on her body, trying to keep my shit together.

"Are you okay?" she asks, reading my expression.

"Am *I* okay? It's you I'm worried about! That bastard put his hands on you and I…I swear to God, I'd fucking kill him if he wasn't already dead!"

Kaylee moves close to me, her hand coming up to cup my face, her eyes holding mine. "He didn't do anything I can't get over, that *we* can't get over, because the other alternative was me being dead. In some ways, it's easier knowing that it wasn't me he wanted, it was Maria. In a weird way, it was like she was protecting me."

I wrap my arms around her, careful of her arm. "I'm here for you. Whatever you need, however long it takes," I promise

"I know," she says, drawing back to look at me. "Now, what does a girl have to do to get you to scrub her back?"

It takes a little inventive towel folding to keep Kaylee's bandaged arm dry, and I take the shower head down so that I can direct the spray to wash her while she sits on the shower seat. She tips her head back as I gently wash her hair, wincing as the water hits the tender spot on her scalp where she hit her head on the stairs.

Finally, the water runs clean, all traces of blood cleansed from her body. I wrap her in a towel, drying her before helping her into a fresh hospital gown and guiding her back to bed.

"Thank you," she sighs, leaning her head back against the pillows I've just plumped behind her, exhausted just from the simple action of showering. She pats the bed next to her and I don't need a second invitation, folding my large frame around her as she rests her head on my chest.

I just hold her, not saying anything, not making promises that everything will be better tomorrow or the next day, knowing that this will be a process of healing and recovery, but that we'll do it together, every step of the way.

KAYLEE
One Week Later

There are only six of us at the graveside, seven including the minister, who has just finished saying a few words as Lev's coffin is lowered into the ground. It's the second funeral I've been to in as many months, three really, as I buried two parents that day, and the pain and heartache threatens to swallow me all over again. How many people can say they've lost four parents in the space of mere weeks?

I'm grateful for the support of Meri on one side of me, holding my hand, and Dawson on the other, his arm around my shoulders. Lev's funeral has been a very understated affair, Daryl wanting to keep it as low key as possible under the circumstances.

I met Daryl and Trish, his fiancée and Prue's Mom, when they came to the house a few days after I was released from the hospital. Daryl is slightly older than Tony, lean with dark hair and ice-blue eyes. At first, I found him a little intimidating, but my nervousness soon disappeared once we got talking and I realized his more serious nature hides a deeply caring side. It's obvious he completely adores Trish, and she him, their love evident every time they look at each other.

Trish is an older version of Prue with the same fiery hair and curvy figure. She pulled me in for a hug the minute we met, telling me how sorry she was for my losses. She's everything I imagine a mother should be, with nurturing nature that wraps around you like a soft blanket.

As we stand at Lev's grave now, Trish, Daryl, Tony, Meri, Dawson and myself, I know that I want to say a few words in recognition of Lev's sacrifice. I take a deep breath, drawing on Dawson and Meri's strength as I take a step forward and start to speak.

"The first time I met Lev I thought he was arrogant and self-absorbed, and my opinion didn't change much the second time I met him," I say, with a wry smile. "He was a flawed man, and nothing can ever excuse the things he did, but I truly believe he started out with good intentions, and in the end, he made the ultimate sacrifice for me. Just before he died…" my voice breaks, and I try to swallow past the lump in my throat, "…he whispered to me that men like him do get second chances at redemption after all. If there's one thing that meeting Lev has taught me, it's that we're not given a good or a bad life, we're simply given a life, and it's up to us to make it good or bad. During our first meeting, I told him that the title of father has to be earned not demanded. So, this is my final gift to you, Lev." Hot tears spill down my cheeks as I bend and place a white lily on top of his coffin. "Rest in peace, daddy."

I stand and turn into the comfort of Dawson's embrace, taking deep breaths as I compose myself.

"We found this photo when we were going through John Grayson's personal belongings and I thought you might like it," Daryl says, coming to stand behind me.

He passes an envelope to Dawson, who opens it for me and my hand flies to my mouth as he pulls out the photo and holds it in front of me.

The woman is beautiful, her long blonde hair curling around her shoulders as she looks down at the baby in her arms, her face so full of love, I can feel it reaching out to me from the faded photograph.

"Oh, wow!" Meri says, coming to stand next to me. "I can see now why Mr. Nutjob thought you were your birth mom! You really do look like her!"

"I can't believe it!" I breathe, as hot tears slip down my cheeks. "I never thought I'd get to see what she looked like. This is amazing. I'll cherish it. Thank you, Daryl!"

"You're welcome. It's the least we could do after all you've been through." Daryl smiles at me as Trish comes to stand next to him, linking her hand with his.

"I'm so sorry for everything Lev put you through," I say to Trish. "Tony told me what he did to you."

Trish gives me one of her warm hugs. "You have nothing to apologise for, Kaylee. Lev was responsible for his own actions, made his own choices, none of which reflect on you, despite what you may think."

"Thank you," I say, squeezing the older woman's hand gratefully. "Prue is very lucky, having a mom like you."

"I'm the lucky one," Trish says, looking up at Daryl with her heart in her eyes.

"Well, I need to head back, chick," Meri says, hugging me. "I'll see you in a few weeks."

"Thanks for coming, honey," I say, returning her hug as tightly as I can with one arm in a sling.

"I'll walk you back to your car," Tony says, and Meri frowns but doesn't say anything, just lifts her arm in a wave, as she and Tony head toward the cemetery parking lot.

Dawson links his fingers through mine. "You need your pain meds," he says, seeing my grimace. "Let's get you home."

As we say our goodbyes to Trish and Daryl, I can't help thinking that Dawson is right - so long as he's with me, this is home for me now.

I'm running as fast as I can, my lungs burning with the effort, and yet I'm not moving. I look down to see my feet are trapped in quicksand and with every movement I make it pulls me down, trying to swallow me whole. I look on with horror as it starts to climb my legs, reaching my hips and then my waist.

Suddenly, Lev appears in front of me, stretching out his arm. "Take my hand, princess!"

My parents appear next to him, holding their hands out to me also and I'm torn, not knowing who to choose.

"You don't need them!" Lev shouts.

"I need you all!" I cry.

"Hurry, Mikhaila! Before he finds us!" Lev pleads.

The sand reaches my chest and I reach out, looking on in horror as I see all the fingers of my hand are missing. I try to scream but my throat muscles are paralysed with terror as I see another figure looming behind Lev. I try to warn him, but it's too late and John plunges a knife into his back…

I jerk awake, the sound of my scream ringing in my own ears, breathing harshly as the nightmare clings to me. The room is in shadow and I panic, trying to escape the sheets that have twisted around my body, my mind still trapped inside the barn.

"It's okay. You're safe." Dawson's voice soothes me instantly, his arms coming around me and I sigh with relief as I remember where I am.

I'm not surprised that my nightmare has returned after Lev's funeral today. For the most part, the pain meds have knocked me out on a night, giving me a blissfully unbroken sleep, but it seems even they weren't able to keep the bad dreams at bay tonight.

"You okay, baby?" Dawson asks, his touch calming me as he brushes my hair back from my face.

"Bad dream. Not surprising after today, I guess," I reply, shakily.

"It's going to take time. I wish I could take all this away from you," he sighs.

I roll onto my good side to face him. "Just having you near me helps."

"Being near you isn't ever going to be a problem," Dawson says, leaning in to kiss me.

"Dawson?" I murmur against his lips.

"Yeah, baby?"

"Make love to me."

Dawson pulls back to look at me, and I can see the uncertainty warring with the desire. "Your arm…"

I throw my leg over his hip, wriggling myself closer and Dawson groans as I press my pussy against his already hard cock. "We'll work around it, baby, but right now I need you. I need your touch, your skin against mine."

Dawson doesn't need any further encouragement and leans forward, brushing his lips softly against mine, his tongue darting out to trace my bottom lip and making me shiver as pleasure snakes through my body. He bites at my mouth as his hands move across my body, trailing his fingers lightly over the dressing on my left arm before sweeping his fingertips around my breasts in torturous circles, almost, but not quite, touching my nipples.

"Dawson!" I moan, my body moving restlessly against him.

"What do you want, Kaylee? Tell me," Dawson demands.

I look into his warm brown eyes, feeling our connection all the way down to my toes. "I want your hands and mouth on me!"

"You got it, baby."

Dawson's thumb finds the hard nub of one breast as he leans down and opens his mouth over the other, sucking hard at my nipple.

"Ah, God, Dawson! That's so good!" I moan, pushing my fingers through his hair and clutching him to me, the scratch of his beard against my skin just heightening the sensation of his mouth on me.

Dawson presses me back into the mattress, resting his weight on his elbows so he doesn't crush me. "Tell me if your arm hurts, okay?" he breathes against my mouth.

"The only thing that hurts is not having you inside me!" I gasp, opening my legs so that the tip of his naked cock presses against my opening.

"Jesus, Kaylee! What are you doing to me?" Dawson growls, as his mouth claims mine in a searing kiss, his tongue pushing inside to tangle with mine.

"Making you mine," I moan, tearing my mouth from his and lifting my hips, encouraging him to fill me with his swollen shaft.

"I've been yours from the moment I saw you outside the prison, maybe even before that," Dawson whispers, his eyes telling me the truth of his words as he slowly begins to merge his body with mine. "I love you, Kaylee, in ways that haven't even been thought of yet!"

"I love you too, Dawson, so much!" I gasp, wrapping my legs around his hips and pressing my feet against the back of his thighs to pull him even deeper inside me, sighing at the exquisite sensation of having him buried so deeply within me.

Dawson looks into my eyes as pulls out of me slowly, creating a sweet drag as he does so and when he thrusts back inside me it's hard to know which one of us moans the loudest. His body creates a soft tempo with mine and I lift my hips to meet the unhurried thrust of his as he takes his time, making love to me with his eyes as well as his body.

"Faster, Dawson," I pant. "I need more!"

Dawson gives me a wicked smile, teasing me as he thrusts slowly inside me again. I clench my internal muscles around him, squeezing his cock, and the smile falls from his face. He grunts as he buries his face against my neck, giving me exactly what I want as he pounds into me, thrusting harder and faster as my thighs grip his hips.

"That's right, baby! Hard! I want it hard!" I demand, shocked at how abandoned I'm being with him.

"I'm not going to last much longer!" Dawson gasps, and his hand moves between us, finding my clit and stroking it with his thumb. "Cum with me, Kaylee. I want to feel your juices on every inch of me!"

My pussy clenches and my eyes roll back as the pleasure begins to bite into my body, the friction of his cock and his thumb making me writhe and gasp underneath him. Suddenly, it's upon me and I throw my head back, chanting his name over and over as I climax, feeling Dawson pumping into me and hearing his own shout of release as his warm cum spurts deep inside me.

"Fuck!" he gasps, his jaw clenched, the muscles in his neck straining as he grinds himself against me with the strength of his orgasm.

He collapses on his side, pulling me against him and I stroke his face, placing kisses on his eyes, his cheeks, his chin, as we both come down from the amazing high.

"You okay, baby?" Dawson asks, still breathing heavily. "We didn't hurt your arm?"

"Don't know," I mumble, with a grin. "My whole body is still numb from the amazing orgasm you just gave me."

He smiles at me, his fingers digging into my hips and he holds me to him, our bodies still joined. "Give me a few minutes, and I'll give you another!"

KAYLEE
Two Weeks Later

"Do you think they'll like living here?"

Dawson wraps his arm around my shoulder, following my gaze to the house. "I think there's going to be a lot of love and laughter in this home."

"I hope so," I say, softly. "They seem like a great couple. Their twins are adorable."

"Just like you," Dawson says, bending to kiss me.

"You always say the right things," I smile against his mouth. "Are you trying to get in my panties again?"

"Always!" he growls, nipping at my bottom lip.

I sweep my good hand around, grabbing his butt and pulling him against me. "Well, you may like to know that I'm not wearing any today."

Dawson groans as he drops his forehead to mine. "Why did you have to tell me that? We have a four-hour journey before I can get you on a horizontal surface!"

"Maybe we don't need to be horizontal," I moan, sliding my hand along the impressive bulge at the front of his jeans.

"Unless you want me to throw you down on the sidewalk and give the neighbours a show, you really need to stop touching me like that, baby!" Dawson gives me a chaste kiss, grinning as he discreetly adjusts himself before letting me go.

We've come back to Bakersfield to clear out the contents of the house. I decided that selling was the wiser choice, knowing I wouldn't ever want to live here again even if Dawson and I weren't moving in together. Not only have I sold the house, but I also had an offer on the accountancy business from one of the senior accountants that worked for Dad. He even wants to keep the name Kemp Accountancy to continue the good reputation Dad built over the years. The sale of both the house and the business means I can support myself financially through veterinary school which I've hope to start in the fall.

Dawson and I have spent an emotional few days sorting through Mom and Dad's stuff, arranging for most of it to go into storage as I'm not ready to donate or sell it yet, but keeping a few sentimental items along with my clothes and personal belongings to take back to Modesto with us. It was a task I was dreading, but having Dawson with me has made the whole process bearable.

Meri was going to come and help us pack everything up too, but she called me a yesterday to say she was sick with a stomach flu. I offered to go and see her, but she asked me not to, saying she didn't want to 'pass on the barf-bug'. She hasn't been herself for a few weeks now and it's obvious something is troubling her, but I know pushing her will only make her clam up even more. I've learned over the years that Meri will come to me when she's ready to talk and not before.

It's sad to think I'm an orphan now, and nothing can take away the loss of my parents, both adoptive and birth, but it's a good feeling having things finally fall into place after having them fall apart for so long. And Dawson's been with me every step of the way, helping me sift through the piles of paperwork and online forms and helping me with my physical therapy exercises. He's been there when I've ugly cried and when I've woken up screaming from a nightmare.

Every day, I fall a little more in love with him and thank whatever fate brought him back into my life.

Things have moved quickly between Dawson and I, but any doubts I had about us moving in together disappeared after my ordeal with John Grayson. I know what I want and that's Dawson, and every look, every touch, tells me he feels the same. It's true that good things come to those who wait but it's also true that great things happen all at once. And Dawson is, without a doubt, the greatest thing that's ever happened to me.

Now I get chance to move forward with my life, with Dawson, but there's just one more thing I need to do before we leave Bakersfield.

"How did it go?" Dawson asks, as I climb back into the Corvette.

"Good. Really good. She and Jake were a little shocked to see me on the doorstep, but Trish must have told Prue everything that's happened because she just grabbed me and hugged me before I'd even finished apologising," I say, giving Dawson a relieved smile.

Trish had given me Prue's address when I told her what I wanted to do. She also told me that it wasn't necessary, that Prue isn't one to hold a grudge, but it was something I needed to do to make things right.

"I said how sorry I was for the way I acted, for the things I said and that I was in a really bad place then. I think they could see that I'm not the same person who waltzed into Jake's apartment a month ago."

"You never were that person, Kaylee. You were angry and hurting. The kind, caring, compassionate woman never went away when your parents died, she just got lost for a little while, but she's always been in here," Dawson says, tapping his fingers against my chest. "I know, because that's the woman I fell in love with. The woman I'm *in love* with."

"Do you have any idea how much I want to fuck you right now?" I grin, pulling his head down to mine.

Dawson smiles against my mouth. "And I thought romance was dead."

DAWSON

The ride home is torture, my mouth watering at the knowledge that Kaylee's sweet pussy is bare under those skin-tight sports leggings she's wearing. Twice, I thought about pulling over to the side of the road, dragging her into my lap and tugging them down so I can bury myself inside her tight hole. The idea of having her ride me in the driver's seat of the Corvette has my cock straining painfully against the confines of my jeans and the only thing stopping me from fulfilling my little fantasy is the lack of privacy on the side of the highway – no one gets to see my woman like that apart from me.

So, instead I content myself with holding her hand where it's resting against my leg as the Corvette eats up the miles. The closer we get to home, the higher her hand inches up my thigh until it settles over the bulge of my erection as she strokes me through my jeans. I turn to look at her with a growl, finding her gaze already on me. Our eyes lock, and I swear a surge of desire shimmers between us, making my breath catch in my throat. A flush stains her cheeks, her blue eyes hooded with desire as she removes her hand from my hard-on and slips it into the front of her leggings.

I swallow hard, trying not to crash the car as Kaylee moves her hand back and forth, and I imagine her sliding her finger between the folds of her slick pussy as she plays with her clit.

"Are you wet, baby?" I growl.

"Mmmm, so wet. Just the way you like me. I want you so badly," she breathes, her eyes closing and her head falling back against the headrest as she moans, grinding herself against her hand.

"I want a taste," I demand, turning the car into our gated community and she lifts her hand to my mouth, moaning again as I draw her finger into my mouth, licking it clean.

We're out of the Corvette the second I park out front of the house, tumbling through the front door, hands tearing at clothing as I back her up against the wall.

Kaylee's nipples are straining against the material of her t-shirt and I rip it down the front, unclipping her bra and spilling her tits into my mouth so I can suckle her there until she gasps my name.

I make short work of the rest of our clothing, helping her ease her arm from her sling so that we're both naked. Before I can think, Kaylee drops to her knees in front of me, taking my engorged shaft in her mouth, her hands circling around to grab my ass and I can feel her fingernails digging into the firm flesh as she holds me to her. My body jerks as she circles her tongue around the end of my cock, swiping back and forth across the sensitive head, before sucking me fully into the warmth of her mouth. She can't fit all of me, but goddamn if she isn't giving it all she's got!

"Fuck, baby!" I grunt, as her mouth works its magic, sucking and pulling at me and I can't help the little thrusts of my hips toward her mouth, feeling my balls start to draw up with my approaching orgasm. "I'm gonna cum, baby!"

Kaylee releases my cock, running her tongue along the underside as she looks up at me. "I want you to cum in my mouth. I want to taste you like you tasted me."
Holy mother of shit, if that's not the hottest thing I've ever heard! She takes me in her mouth again, her lips sealing around me firmly as she moves her mouth back and forth, back and forth, using her talented tongue in ways I could never have imagined.

"Agh! God!" I throw my head back and roar as I cum hard and fast, my semen unloading in thick spurts into her mouth, my pleasure almost endless as she continues to lick at me until my knees almost buckle.

Kaylee stands, pressing her naked body against mine as she pulls my head down, kissing me deeply so that I can taste myself on her lips.

"Jesus, woman! You just about blew my fucking balls off!" I breathe, against her mouth.

"You looked as if you enjoyed it," she grins, looking at me from underneath her lashes.

"Enjoy doesn't quite cover it, baby. Now, it's my turn!"

Kaylee squeals as I sweep her off her feet and into my arms, carrying her to the sofa and sitting down so she's straddling my lap. My eyes rake up and down her body, taking in her glorious tits with their rosy nipples, her narrow waist and long legs. My eyes settle on her pussy and I rein in the urge to slide my fingers through the neat triangle of dark blonde hair that now covers it, wanting something else, right now.

"I want to see you touch yourself again." I lean back against the cushions behind me, almost drooling on myself as I watch her slide her hand down her body, opening her puffy lips and easing a finger into her wet folds. Her body jerks involuntarily as she stimulates her clit and the sight is so fucking hot I can feel myself swelling again. Someone needs to tell my cock that it's too soon after the blistering orgasm she just gave me, but it seems he's always hungry for this woman of mine.

"You're so wet, I can see your juices coating your fingers. Does it feel good, baby?" I ask, my voice hoarse.

"So good!" she moans. "It never felt like this when I did it before. It's you. It's what you do to me, how you make me feel."

I lean forward, sucking a nipple into my mouth and flicking the hard nub with my tongue before giving the other one the same treatment, loving the taste of her soft skin. Kaylee mewls and writhes above me as her fingers continue to work on her clit. I sweep a hand down to join hers, sliding a finger inside her and she rocks against me, her breathing harsh and her pupils dilated as she gets close to her climax.

"You're close, baby. Make that pretty pussy purr for me and cum all over my fingers." I hook my finger around, pressing against the little patch of rough skin inside her and she flies over the edge, throwing her head back and chanting my name over and over like a litany, her body straining with the intensity of her release, before collapsing breathlessly against me.

I nuzzle my face into her neck, trailing my lips across her shoulder and gently kissing the scars that are still healing at the top of her arm. Kaylee sighs contentedly, lifting her head to look at me and a wave of pure love passes between us that transcends words.

She leans in, kissing me softly as she slowly sinks down onto my cock, jerking as her still sensitive flesh rubs against my pubic bone. Her tongue slides against mine as she works her hips up and down, pausing at the top and working just the head of my cock in and out of her wet channel. I grasp her hips, wanting more and she drops all the way down on me, both of us moaning at the sensation as her pussy sucks me in to the hilt.

Kaylee whimpers in disappointment as I lift her off me, flipping her onto her back and kneeling in front of her as I hook her legs over my shoulders.

I plunge into her again, the position allowing me to go deeper than ever before and Kaylee's eyes roll back as I bottom out inside her, arching her body to meet me as I pull out and sink into her again and again, each thrust of my hips bumping against her clit. The loud, wet sounds of our bodies coming together turns me on even more and I increase my pace, sliding my hands down her legs to brace her hips as I pound into her.

"You're all mine!" I gasp, feeling the delicious tingle in my balls as I get close.

"I'm yours, Dawson! Always!" Kaylee whimpers, her eyes holding mine as I surge into her and her body spasms, her pussy contracting around me as she releases her sticky juices all over my cock.

With one last grunt, I follow her, riveting my hips against her as I empty my seed deep inside her, choking out her name as my body is held in a rictus of pleasure.

It takes a long time for me to catch my breath and I'm in no rush to pull out of Kaylee's soft body. I could stay like this forever, relishing the feeling of closeness, but she shifts uncomfortably underneath me and although she doesn't say anything, I know her arm is aching.

"Don't go," she pouts, as I move away from her.

"Don't move. I'll be right back," I say, and her eyes cling to me as I make my way upstairs.

I grab what I need from our room, returning downstairs as Kaylee emerges from the downstairs bathroom.

I throw a duvet over the sofa and Kaylee snuggles underneath while I grab her pain meds and a glass of water from the kitchen, handing her both and watching as she swallows the pills.

"What's that?" she asks, pointing to the package wrapped in silver paper that I placed on the coffee table.

"A present." I smile and pass it to her, climbing under the duvet and positioning her so she's leaning back against me.

"A present? But it's not my birthday for another few weeks," she says, surprised.

"I know, but I wanted you to have this now."

Kaylee tugs at the wrapping paper, tears spilling down her cheeks as she reveals the silver frame with its photograph.

"I had the photo enlarged and enhanced," I say, softly.

Kaylee throws her arms round my neck, grimacing as the movement jars her arm. "I love it! It's beautiful! Thank you!" She kisses me hard, snuggling back against me as her eyes move lovingly over the picture of her mother cradling her in her arms, a soft smile pulling at her lips.

"One day, that will be you holding our child," I murmur, watching her face flush with pleasure at the thought.

Kaylee leans forward and carefully places the frame on the coffee table before wriggling to face me, her hands dropping beneath the duvet and trailing down my abs, making my cock twitch to life again.

"In that case, we'd better do some more practising," she whispers as her lips descend on mine.

I have a feeling our 'practising' is going to take us long into the night.

Read on for an excerpt from Playing Dirty, Book 3 of the Play Series.

DARYL

Nothing prepared me for the sight of her in the flesh. She took my breath away from the moment I walked into the diner a month ago. Her natural beauty instantly drew my gaze and her warmth pulled me to her like a magnet.

She'd seemed nervous that first morning and had spilled coffee all over the table while she was refilling my cup, apologising profusely as she tried to mop it up. Her flush of embarrassment and the tremor of her hands had only increased the instant attraction I felt for her.

On impulse, I'd reached across and placed my hand over hers, stilling her frantic movements. I can still feel the electricity that crackled between us as her green eyes lifted to mine, a mixture of surprise and uncertain desire in them at the physical contact. We'd stayed like that, our gazes locked, until another customer asking for a refill had interrupted the moment, causing Trish to tear her eyes away from mine.

I'd asked her to join me for coffee during her break that first morning. It seemed like the perfect opportunity to set the ball in motion to obtain the information I need. Every morning since, she's joined me during her break and every day my feelings for her have grown.

I keep telling myself that my interest in her is purely professional, but the truth is I like being near her. I never imagined how much I would look forward to our time together. I wanted to learn more about her, about the real woman behind the dry facts contained in her file.

The thick folder tells me everything I need to know about her on a professional level, but it doesn't reveal the real essence of the woman, what makes her tick. The flat and grainy photographs it contains don't do justice to the way her face becomes animated when she's excited or the infectious laughter that accompanies her million-watt smile and lights up the room around her.

The file tells me that her name is Patricia Daniels, but not that everyone calls her Trish.

It tells me she's about to turn forty years old, but not that her smooth, blemish free skin means she could pass for a woman much younger.

I know she has a daughter, Prudence, but the file doesn't reveal the depth of the love she has for her only child.

It reveals that she helped put two men behind bars, one of which is her now ex-husband but says nothing of the horror she must have felt coming home to find Diego Martinez trying to rape her teenage daughter while her husband cowered in a corner, high on heroin.

No, these are all things I've learned while we've talked and laughed over coffee, and with each day that passes I'm becoming more and more lost in her.

My gaze is drawn to her again as I watch her serve a couple at another booth. I notice how strands of her vibrant red hair have escaped from the loose bun she wears it in and how the curls frame her lovely face. I'm fascinated by the way her eyes crinkle and the little dimples that appear in her cheeks when she smiles or laughs. I want to lick those dimples and claim her lips with mine, open her mouth to my tongue so I can taste her sweetness.

I know she's been single since her divorce and on first learning this I was surprised to find myself relieved. The thought of another man in her life triggers an unwarranted jealousy. It's hard to believe a woman like her would still be single, that some man hasn't snapped her up and made her his in the years since her divorce.

Not that it matters because she's off limits. I keep reminding myself that I'm in no position to make a move on her, that I'm here to do a job, nothing more, nothing less. The problem is, my mission has shifted from business to personal, a dangerous change of priorities in my line of work. I can't tell her that she's part of the reason I'm here. Hopefully I won't have to if today goes as planned.

I've tried to ignore the physical pull I feel toward her but every day the tension between us seems to ratchet up another notch to the point where all I want now is to bend her back over the table, spread her legs and ease the ache she's ignited in my body between her soft thighs.

I sense her approaching my table now, so attuned am I to her presence. I look up and those vivid green eyes of hers steal my breath. I know I could lose myself in them if I look too long but I can't tear my eyes away. I notice the increased rise and fall of her breasts, her flushed cheeks, and can't help the silent satisfaction I feel at knowing she's as attracted to me as I am to her.

"More coffee, Daryl?"

The sound of my name on her lips is like an aphrodisiac and I wonder what it would be like to hear her scream it as I make her orgasm. The mental image instantly makes me hard and I'm grateful for the table which covers the blatant evidence of my arousal.

I nod in answer to her question and notice again the slight tremble of her hand as she refills my cup, telling me that she's as affected by our proximity as I am.

"Can I get you anything else?"

Now there's a question and a half. I can think of a whole multitude of things I'd like her to get me right now that aren't on the menu.

"No thanks, Trish." I hold her eyes with a smile. I'm not known for my outgoing personality but with her my smile seems to come easily.

"How's the book going?" Trish indicates the notebook on the table in front of me, referring to my cover story that I'm an author taking time out to write my latest novel.

"Well, as you can see, the words aren't exactly flowing today," I grimace, turning the notebook so she can see the blank screen.

"Hmmm. I think we need to get some inspiration for you from somewhere. It's a thriller, right?" Trish asks.

"Yeah, but nothing particularly thrilling is happening right now, apart from talking to you, of course." I grin, watching the flush that settles over her cheeks. My eyes drop to her mouth as her lips part and her tongue darts out to moisten them. Holy fuck, that's hot!

"Oh, I think you definitely need something more thrilling than that for your book," Trish jokes. "Maybe, I'm really a spy, undercover on a secret operation!" She waggles her eyebrows at me.

My laughter sounds forced as her innocent words hit too close to home. "I think I'll leave the spy stuff to Ian Fleming," I chuckle.

Trish sighs dramatically. "Oh well, it was worth a try," she grins. "Just give me a holler if you need a refill."

I watch the sexy sway of her hips under her waitress uniform as she walks away. Does she know how perfect her ass is? How much I'd like to back her up against a wall somewhere and sink into her soft body?

Hell! I need to get a grip. I need to get my mind off her delectable curves and focus on the job at hand.

The feelings this woman engenders has me all kinds of unsettled. There's a vulnerability about Trish that brings out a part of me that wants to beat my chest, drag her to my man cave and protect her. I tell myself I'm too fucking old for this crap, that I've seen too much of the shitty side of life to believe in the concept of instant attraction or love at first sight.

In the past, my personal relationships have been few and far between and although I've wanted women, I've never *needed* them. Any intimacy with the opposite sex has been for the sole purpose of scratching an itch, nothing more. I've managed to reach the grand old age of forty-two avoiding any form of emotional commitment, no major love affairs, happy with my own company for the most part. Not to mention it would take a special kind of woman to accept the work I do, the risks involved and the kind of people I deal with.

I glance down at my watch. I need to get going. The diner has been the ideal place to gain Trish's trust as well as familiarize myself with the area. There's a lot riding on the success of this latest deal and I can't afford any fuck ups.

I toss a twenty on the table and stand to leave, pulling on my leather jacket. My movement catches her eye and I can feel the heat of her gaze as she looks at me, taking in everything from my booted feet and low-slung jeans to the black t-shirt beneath the jacket. It's all I can do to control the reaction of my body to her curious gaze. Whatever this thing is with her it's messing with my head and I can't afford the distraction. I need to keep my wits about me.

I quickly make my exit and head down the alley that runs alongside the diner, pulling up the collar of my jacket to keep the chill autumn wind at bay.

As I 'round the corner, I see the two men already waiting for me. There's an air of menace about them which others might find intimidating, but I can hold my own. I'm no lightweight at six three and two hundred pounds and I keep myself in good shape. I have to, because in my world, it could be the difference between surviving and not.

"I'm glad to see you are a man who values punctuality," the larger of the two men says with a thick Spanish accent.

"Guillermo," I nod, reaching out to shake the hand he extends toward me. Although we're similar in height, he's built like a brick shithouse, all heavy muscles and swarthy complexion. His dark hair is slicked back from his face, his expression guarded as his eyes narrow on me.

"Make sure our guest isn't carrying, Rodrigo."

I hold my jacket open as his colleague, a shorter guy with dirty blonde hair, steps forward to pat me down. I'm relying on him not doing a thorough job because I have my HK45 stashed in my boot.

"You have the money?" Guillermo asks.

I pull the wad of used bills from the inside pocket of my jacket, holding it up so he can see but not handing it to him. "I wanna see the goods," I demand.

Guillermo doesn't move for a full minute as he looks me up and down and I'm just starting to think we may have a problem when he gives a brief nod to his companion.

Rodrigo reaches into the car and pops the trunk open and I walk to the other side of the car, keeping my back to the wall behind me and my line of sight open so that no one can come up the alley without me knowing about it. Why the fuck Guillermo wanted to do the drop here, in such a confined space, I'll never know.

"It's all there," Guillermo assures me as I reach in to unzip the black holdall. As I'm lifting out one of the packets, the sound of a door opening causes all three of us to whip toward the source of the noise.

Shit! My stomach drops as Trish exits backward through the service door of the diner, struggling with a large bag of garbage. She doesn't see us straight away, absorbed as she is in her task, but as she turns, she stops short, her mouth making a silent 'O' as her eyes round in surprise.

"What the fuck?" Guillermo comes toward me, snatching the package from my hand and dropping it into the trunk before slamming it closed. But it's too late. She's already seen enough, and I know that she's figured out exactly what's going on.

"I'll deal with it," I growl, putting an arm out to block Guillermo, who's about to move toward Trish.

I stride toward her, the fear I expect to see in her eyes absent. Instead, her expression is one of disgust and ... disappointment, which makes me feel as if I've somehow failed her in some way despite her not knowing all the facts.

Before she can move, I've gathered her up against me and my lips come crashing down on hers, my tongue pushing into her mouth. I tell myself that it's got to look convincing, but the truth is, it's all too easy to get lost in her sweet mouth, the softness of her lips.

I tangle my hands through her hair and press her back into the wall behind her, my body covering hers protectively as I deepen the kiss, almost forgetting where we are.

I tear my mouth from hers, moving my lips to her ear. "You need to do exactly what I say. Go back inside, close the door and stay there."

My words are a caress that only she can hear and as I draw back to look into her eyes, I see shock, and now the fear, that was missing moments ago

For a few long, seconds, she doesn't move but then she gives a jerky nod before making a hasty retreat through the door she came out of, closing it quietly behind her. I release a breath and turn back to face Guillermo.

"She your woman?" Guillermo asks in his thick accent, his eyes unusually intense. His mouth lifts in a smirk as I nod abruptly. "Shame. Would've liked a little piece of that pussy for myself, know what I mean?"

I grit my teeth at the thought of him putting his filthy hands on Trish. "Let's get this done," I growl, ignoring his words and moving back toward the car. I pull the money from my jacket and hand it to Guillermo and Rodrigo opens the trunk again.

As I bend over to retrieve the holdall I feel the cold metal of a gun muzzle pressed against the back of my head.

"Do you think I was born yesterday you stupid fuck?" Guillermo's voice is heavy with anger.

"You think I don't know a cop when I see one? The fucking stink is all over you!"

I curse inwardly, knowing I've just made a mistake worthy of a rookie, that I've allowed myself to be distracted by certain redhead and put us both in danger.

My mind goes into overdrive as I consider my options. I need to stall for time, but my odds are not good. Even if I can take Guillermo out, that still leaves his companion.

I have no choice but to try and bluff my way out. "Put the gun down, Guillermo. Whatever the fuck you think you know, you really don't!"

"You think you're the first *pendejo* that's tried to take me down? *No me jodas*, motherfucker! Nobody shafts me, you understand? Nobody!"

I hear the click of the gun cocking and close my eyes, knowing I'm about to become another statistic with a bullet in his brain.

24415104R00145

Printed in Great Britain
by Amazon